They had targets on their backs.

And there was no way he'd let her come with him straight into the gang's den.

"We're partners, Trent," Chloe said.

"Not anymore."

She opened the door and stood there in full motorcycle gear. "You think I've never walked into a room full of criminals who'd kill me as soon as look at me?"

He shook his head. "My plan—"

"Your plan is going to get you killed," she said, cutting him off. "You think they'll really believe you're so irresistible that you charmed a dedicated detective into spilling classified information without her knowledge?"

"I don't have any choice."

"Yes, you do." Her hands snapped to her hips. "Here's my plan. I walk in there and do what I don't believe you can. Convince a room full of killers that I sold out my badge for you. That I'm your fiancée and that I've fallen head over heels for you." She stepped closer and trailed a finger down his cheek. "Because if I don't, we're both dead."

Maggie K. Black is an award-winning journalist and romantic suspense author with an insatiable love of traveling the world. She has lived in the American South, Europe and the Middle East. She now makes her home in Canada with her history-teacher husband, their two beautiful girls and a small but mighty dog. Maggie enjoys connecting with her readers at maggiekblack.com.

Visit the Author Profile page at Harlequin.com.

UNDERCOVER HOLIDAY FIANCÉE

MAGGIE K. BLACK

HARLEQUIN® LOVE INSPIRED® SUSPENSE

Recycling programs for this product may not exist in your area.

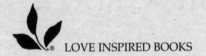

LOVE INSPIRED BOOKS

ISBN-13: 978-0-373-45744-1

Undercover Holiday Fiancée

Copyright © 2017 by Mags Storey

www.Harlequin.com

Printed in U.S.A.

"Come now, let us settle the matter," says the Lord.
"Though your sins are like scarlet,
they shall be as white as snow."
—Isaiah 1:18

In memory of my grandfather, who taught me
how to tell stories, and my grandmother, who taught me
how to laugh. I miss you and I hope I made you proud.

Thanks as always to my agent, Melissa Jeglinski,
my editor, Emily Rodmell, and the rest of
the Love Inspired team, who encourage authors like me
and bring stories like these to life.

ONE

The crash of exploding glass echoed up through the empty halls of the Bobcaygeon Sports Center, shattering the early morning peace and drowning out the melody of Christmas carols. Moments earlier, Ontario Provincial Police Detective Chloe Brant had been running in place as a treadmill cycled endlessly beneath her. Now she heard shouting. She yanked the treadmill's emergency cord and grabbed the handles for stability as the belt shuddered to a stop beneath her feet. Her steady green eyes looked through the interior window of the sports center's second-floor exercise room down at the lobby below, just in time to see a skinny figure in a rubber elf mask knock over the Christmas tree with the wild swing of a baseball bat.

What's happening, Lord? What do I do to help?

The large window that had encased the front desk had been bashed in and was now a cobweb of shards held together by nothing but safety-glass coating. The first elf was joined by a second, who was holding a knife and seemed equally intent on mindless destruction, stomping on tree ornaments as they rolled across the floor.

At five thirty in the morning, the center was so deserted that the front desk and the coffee counter hadn't even been staffed when she'd headed up to the exercise room. Hopefully that just meant destruction and chaos—not actual casualties.

If gossip around her police division was true, local Trillium Community College—where Chloe herself had spent a year over a decade ago—had a major drug problem the Bobcaygeon police were completely failing to deal with. Accidental overdoses had spiked last spring. A baggie containing thousands of dollars' worth of a new designer pill, nicknamed "payara," had turned up in the sports center locker room. Now, vice units across the country were hearing about payara being trafficked, in small amounts, through their own communities' criminal networks. Seemed whoever was creating it was testing Canada's appetite for a new illegal way to get high.

Some said local staff sergeant, Frank Butler, was going to find himself facing a major internal investigation if he didn't figure out where the drugs were coming from, and fast. Butler had been Chloe's first training officer. He was in his late sixties and, while they'd never been close, she had attended his wife's funeral two years earlier and now hated the thought of a dedicated officer's reputation being destroyed so close to the end of his career. Even if he had made a mistake, he deserved an opportunity to get help and fix it. Not to mention that if he was embroiled in a scandal, it could tarnish her own career and sabotage the promotion to detective sergeant she'd been striving for. She had a week off for Christmas and a house less than an hour away. She'd emailed Butler, asking if there was anything she could do to help. He hadn't answered.

Chloe was the kind of person who took action while praying. So, for the past three days, she'd been scouting the sports center, just exercising, observing and asking God for guidance—never expecting the first hint of trouble she'd spot would come in the form of masked elves brazenly destroying the place.

Gang violence, probably. Especially considering the drug connection. Most ordinary criminals weren't that brazen.

She glanced back toward the exercise room. There were two other people in there and both seemed to be college students. The blond jock on the treadmill was wearing a jersey from nearby rival college: Haliburton. He'd introduced himself as Johnny when he'd first walked in and made a cocky attempt at impressing her with some tale of being a tech genius and entrepreneur before quickly moving on to flirting with the dark-haired young woman on the rowing machine. Now both of them were staring in her direction.

She yanked her badge out of her sweatshirt and held it up on its lanyard. "Stay there. Don't move."

Before they could answer, she slipped off the treadmill and crept along the window for a better view of what was happening below. The faint outline of her reflection mirrored back at her. Six feet tall and lithe, she might've been mistaken for some kind of athlete.

But with her long, flaming red hair often scraped back into a bun, she knew the overall impression she usually gave was more of a librarian, especially since she'd reached her midthirties.

The scene shifted below her. She saw a third, bulky elf shove the elderly security guard up against a wall as the shape of a young woman cowered behind Nanny's Coffee counter. There was a gun in the elf's hand. Chloe turned back to the students.

"I'm Detective Chloe Brant, OPP." Her voice rang with authority. "There's a disturbance on the main floor. At least three armed intruders wearing elf masks. I'm going to check it out. You're both going to stay here and lock the door." She pointed to the young woman, making the snap judgment she'd be the more responsible of the two. "What's your name?"

"Poppy." Her dark eyes were filled with fear but her voice was strong. "Did you say elves?"

"Yes, elves." If this was somebody's idea of a sick holiday joke, Chloe wasn't laughing. "Poppy, please call 9-1-1. Johnny, look for ways to barricade the door."

But the young woman was staring at her. "I know you, right? You're dating one of my teachers. I think I saw your picture at the college."

"Focus, Poppy!" Chloe ignored the ridiculous question. She'd assumed Poppy would be the better choice. It never ceased to amaze her how people's brains seized up in shock. Relationships might be top of the mind for these young people but they were the last thing on hers. "I need you to call 9-1-1. Hand me the phone when they answer." She held out her hand and waited while Poppy dialed.

She took the phone, gave Dispatch her name, badge number, cell phone number and a concise description of the situation. Then she handed the phone back to Poppy. "Stay on the line with them and answer their questions. They'll tell you what to do."

"But my boyfriend's on the Trillium hockey team," Poppy said. "He's at the rink setting up the Christmas toy mountain with the coach and Third Line."

Chloe took a deep breath. Okay, so that potentially meant even more people in danger. She'd spotted the dark hair and rather hunky broad shoulders of the bearded college coach pass by with a handful of players yesterday, but he'd left before she'd made her way downstairs or gotten a good look at him. "Don't worry. I'll make sure they get out okay. What's Third Line?"

"It's the group of guys on a hockey team who hit the ice third," Johnny said. "If they get to play at all, because they're not as good as first- or second-line players. I play first line for Haliburton." His tone implied he'd never be caught dead playing anything else. He stepped off the treadmill. "I'll go with you."

"No, you won't," she said. "Not unless you're a cop or military. Are you?"

"No, but a friend of mine is." His chin rose.

Right, and her sister was a journalist and her father was a con man.

"Stay here with Poppy," she told him. "Lock the door behind me and stay away from the windows."

She slipped out of the exercise room. The door

clicked shut behind her. Her feet moved silently down the hallway, her fingers aching for her service weapon. But this was Canada and so, because she was off duty, her gun was in her car, safely unloaded and locked away.

She paused at the top of the stairs and looked down at the shards of red and gold glass spread across the floor below. She pulled out her phone, turned it on and made sure the ringer was on silent. It buzzed with a Missed Call notification. She glanced at it. Apparently she'd missed a call almost an hour ago. It was from a blocked number, but she was so sure she knew who it was from, his name might as well have filled the screen. *Trent*.

Detective Trent Henry of the Royal Canadian Mounted Police was one of the nation's finest undercover detectives. Strong and rugged, with the kind of heart-melting blue eyes that hinted at a familiarity with danger, they'd worked together three times so far. They always clicked so well, she'd expected they'd stay in touch. But each time he'd dropped out of her life without even saying goodbye.

Then, suddenly, he'd called her a handful of times in the past two weeks, with the same curt and blunt demand. "Call me. We should get coffee." No, thanks. She didn't take orders from men like Trent, no matter how rugged their jawlines or how stellar their reputations. Not that she didn't wish Trent was with her now. When she'd met him, he'd been undercover with the province's most notorious gang, the Wolfspiders. Nobody knew more about Canada's drug and gang operations than Trent Henry.

She reached the bottom of the stairs. The hallway

was empty. She crept over to the coffee counter and crouched down. A pair of huge and frightened brown eyes looked up at her. The girl was wearing a black shirt and an apron that advertised Nanny's Diner and Coffee. Her face was vaguely familiar in a way Chloe couldn't immediately place. Her name tag read Lucy.

Chloe raised her badge. "I'm Detective Chloe Brant and it's going to be okay. Where are the elves?"

"The ice rink." Lucy's voice barely rose above a whisper. "They asked the security guard where it was. The guard escaped. But I stayed hidden."

"Probably smart," Chloe said. "How about the players and the coach?"

"They're hiding outside the rink, including my brother." Lucy held up her phone. It showed a string of messages from someone named Brandon. The contact picture was a slender young man with a nervous smile. "But the elves have their coach. They're going to kill him."

"Not if I can help it," Chloe said. If the elves were hunting hockey players, she hoped Johnny had done what he was told and stayed in the exercise room. She could hear footsteps in the distance now. Sounded like one of the elves was on his way back. "I need you to run out of here as fast as you can and don't look back."

Lucy hesitated.

"Hey!" A voice filled the air to her right. Chloe turned. It was the hefty elf. A knife flashed in his hand.

"Run!" Chloe sprang to her feet. "Don't stop until you're safe!"

The elf charged. Lucy ran. Chloe threw herself between them. She dodged as the knife slashed through the air inches from her stomach. She grabbed his wrist to wrench the knife from his grasp, but his wet boots slipped on the tiled floor. He fell backward. Chloe landed on top of him. The knife flashed in front of her eyes. She leveled a blow to his jaw, snapping his head back against the floor. As she twisted the knife from his hand, she noticed his tattooed wrist read GGB. It was a gang sign for the Gulo Gulo Boys.

The Gulo wrenched himself from her grasp, leaped up and ran after Lucy.

Chloe sprinted after him, ready to tackle him if that's what it took to help the young woman escape.

She heard a clatter and watched as his cell phone bounced across the floor behind him. *Gotcha!* She scooped up the phone, spun around and ran for the stairs. A roar of anger left his throat as he realized what she'd done. She almost smiled. A gang member was nothing without his phone. She sprinted up the stairs to the second floor, hearing his footsteps pound after her.

"Give me back my phone!" he bellowed, his voice echoing through the stairwell. "Or I'll kill you!"

She lead him in the opposite direction of the exercise room, dodged behind a pillar and then turned sharply to head down a side hall toward the hockey rink. Had he seen where she'd gone? She didn't know if he had another weapon on him and didn't much want to find out. She ducked behind a Christmas tree and gasped in a breath, just long enough to look over the railing. The round foyer in front of the hockey rink lay beneath her, complete with a wooden platform stage and a giant mountain of stuffed animals towering almost all the way up to the second floor.

Four figures lay flat on their stomachs under the stage, their shadowy outlines barely visible through the slats below. But, even at a distance, she could recognize the Trillium College hockey jerseys. The two Gulos she'd seen earlier stood between them and freedom. One was swinging his bat at anything he could break. The other stood stock-still, his back to her and a gun in his hand.

Then he shifted and her gaze fell to the man kneeling on the ground in front of him.

It was the coach. The sweet-looking, bearded man was kneeling, his head bowed and hands outstretched, as he placed his life between the hidden students and the gang members. Something about his courage made it impossible for Chloe to look away. She could hear the other Gulo coming down the hallway toward her now. She had to run. She had to fight.

The gang member pressed the barrel of his gun between the coach's eyes, execution style. The coach's chin rose. Then his gaze turned toward her. Keen, piercing blue eyes met hers. Her heart leaped into her throat, stealing a breath from her parted lips.

It was Detective Trent Henry.

Trent's heart sank as his eyes latched onto Chloe's form crouched at the railing above. The feeling of dread in his gut was matched only by the frustration burning at the back of his throat. What was she doing here? First she ignored his calls and then she stumbled into his investigation? He'd called her to get some advice on his undercover assignment over a quick cup of coffee. Getting threatened by weapon-wielding Gulos had never been part of the plan.

Help me, God. This whole drug investigation has been a mess from the start and now it's falling apart around my ears. Help me figure out how to get everyone out of here alive.

If Chloe got killed, or even hurt, he'd never forgive himself. The gun currently pointed between his eyes didn't help matters much. He'd taken out quite a few Gulo operations over the years and the memories were especially vicious. He shuddered to think what it meant that they were staging something so blatant.

Seconds earlier he'd been praying for a diversion. Something simple and straightforward that would enable him to take out two gang members at once in a way that didn't blow either his cover or risk the lives of his hockey players. Now, here the strongest, toughest and most infuriating cop he'd ever known had somehow materialized on the floor above him, making his job that much harder.

Her eyes were now locked on his face. She'd recognized him. He watched as shouts and footsteps suddenly sounded from above, giving Chloe barely moments to leap to her feet before a third Gulo pelted down the hall toward her. Chloe threw her shoulder into the Christmas tree and tossed it at the gang member like a football tackle. The Gulo grunted and fell under the force of pine needles and branches. Trent nearly whistled.

It was a gutsy move and impressive—not that he

didn't wish she'd run instead. But he could tell she'd also seen his players in their hiding place. Had he been right to tell them to hide instead of fight? Hard to know. The four young men weren't the best athletes or experienced fighters. Hodge had gotten a text from his girlfriend, Poppy, saying there were heavily armed criminals swarming the building.

When Trent had heard the chaos and destruction moving through the halls toward them, he'd ordered his players to hide and not a single one had argued. Instead they'd all dived for the narrow crawl space below the platform. Later, he could worry about whether that meant anything to his case. He'd gotten used to thinking of the four of them as his suspects. So it was pretty ironic that a Gulo was now pointing a gun at his face and threatening to kill him if he didn't spill the exact same information he'd spent the last three months completely failing to figure out for himself.

The Gulos wanted to know who was manufacturing the new designer drug and the location of their lab. So did Trent.

After three months of painstaking undercover work as the interim Trillium College hockey coach and sports education teacher, he was absolutely positive that the only people who could've possibly hidden that baggie stuffed with payara pills in the garbage can was one of the four third-line players now hiding under the platform behind him.

He had little doubt that the other three players might very well have coordinated their stories to protect whoever it was. Breaking through their wall of silence and finding out who was his core mission and would be the key to finding the manufacturer and unraveling the entire drug operation. He also knew, without a doubt, that none of the players—whatever their crimes—deserved the vicious evil the Gulos would mete out.

And as of right now, the only two things standing in the way of that was him and the magnificent, glorious, red-haired cop now fighting an armed criminal on the floor above. He watched, with his knees pressed into the floor and his hands raised, as Chloe spun toward the masked Gulo. The thug yanked a knife from his boot and lunged. Her leg shot out hard with a flying roundhouse to kick the weapon from his hand. It slid across the floor and wedged in the railing. The Gulo threw himself at her and then it was a battle of limbs as Chloe and the gang member struggled for dominance.

The masked man standing in front of Trent jabbed the barrel of his weapon into Trent's forehead. "Who's she?"

Now that was a complicated question and a pretty long story. Chloe was a stunning, difficult and complicated woman. The kind that would drive a man crazy if he let her, until he found himself lying awake at night, staring at the cracks in his hotel room ceiling, counting all the ways he wasn't good enough for her.

The gun dug even deeper. "Is she with you?"

"She's not with me," Trent said. "I honestly don't know what she's doing here."

Yes, he'd called her several times, including earlier that very morning. When he'd first taken this case, he hadn't expected it to take more than a few weeks. He'd get the young men to confide in him, find out where the payara had come from, determine if it had a link to the local police division and then an official task force would be formed to take over and investigate further.

In fact, he was supposed to launch into prep for another much larger and longer investigation way up in the Arctic after Christmas. The substitute teacher cover story had seemed ideal. After all, he'd gotten violent gang members and criminals to spill their deepest secrets. How hard could gaining the trust of four college students be? But the real Trillium sports professor and hockey coach was supposed to return from paternity leave after Christmas. Trent's excuse for being in Bobcaygeon and in these players' lives was rapidly ending, and he was no closer to finding the source of the payara.

He'd needed help. He'd needed advice. School had never been his scene. But Chloe had lived in Bobcaygeon. She'd gone to Trillium College. She was book smart. Plus, she'd trained under the very same local staff sergeant who'd either bungled the case or was corrupt enough to be bribed. Trent wasn't sure which it was, all he knew was that there was something off about Frank Butler. The staff sergeant had an agitation that rubbed him the wrong way. Not to mention that one of the third-line players was Butler's grandson, Brandon. Chloe could help, if they all made it out of there alive.

He watched as Chloe tossed the Gulo off and rolled away, out of sight. Her attacker lunged after her. He stared at the empty space above, willing for some kind of sign that Chloe was okay. Sweat formed at his hairline. *Lord God, please don't let her get hurt! Help me get this gun out of my face so I can rescue her and the players!*

A flash of brilliant red filled his view as he watched the Gulo grab Chloe and throw her against the railing. Her hair tumbled free from its bun in long loose waves that trailed down her back. Visceral pain pierced his chest as Chloe's head snapped back. The Gulo lifted her by the throat and tried to force her backward over the railing. Every muscle in Trent's limbs tensed to fight even as he felt the barrel of a gun holding him in place. If he got shot in the head, he was no use to her. But he couldn't just kneel there and watch as she got hurt. He'd learned when he was thirteen what could happen if he let somebody down. The death of his only sister had been a very high price to pay.

That was it. He'd risk the bullet. He pushed to his feet.

"Get back down!" the Gulo in front of him ordered.

Trent stared into the bland, lifeless eyes behind the mask.

"You think I won't kill you? You think you're gonna save your own skin by not telling me where your players are? You know one of them is dealing payara?"

Well, Trent knew one of them had tossed the pills in the trash. But he wasn't convinced that meant they were an actual drug dealer. Sure the third-line players each had their problems but none had struck him as gang potential. He'd know. He'd been fourteen and still angrily grieving the murder of his sister when the Wolfspiders had tried to tangle him into their web. And that was a secret about himself he'd keep to his grave.

"We're here looking for payara!" The Gulo holding Trent hostage raised his voice. "Tell us where the lab is and who's been making it. Or I'm gonna shoot your coach between the eyes."

Trent gritted his teeth and prayed. Chloe's feet kicked futilely in the air as her attacker lifted her higher over the railing. If only he'd solved this case earlier, none of this would've ever happened and Chloe wouldn't be in this position.

God, please, don't let Chloe die because of my failure.

Then a scream, bordering on a warrior yell, filled the air above him as Chloe flew backward over the railing.

TWO

Chloe's body tumbled through the air. She tucked her head into her knees, braced herself for impact and aimed for the huge mountain of stuffed toys. The second she'd felt herself about to go over the railing she'd kicked the gang member in the chest with both feet and launched herself out of his hands. If that criminal had been so determined to force her backward, she was going to take charge of the moment. Life had taught her that much. She couldn't always control whether or not she was going to fall. But she could control how she landed.

Her body hit the mound of fluffy stuffed animals, just like a kid cannonballing into a ball pit, sending toys flying. She gasped a prayer. Then she reached for her pocket and breathed a sigh of relief. She still had the Gulo's cell phone.

She pushed her way up through the mound and looked at Trent. He was still down on his knees, with the barrel of a gun against his skin, and his face pale as he scanned for her. Her gaze met his and a visible wave of relief swept over him.

But still she could read the question floating in his blue eyes.

She nodded, feeling the sliver of a smile brush her lips.

He grinned and turned back to the Gulo, who was staring at Chloe in shock. Trent struck. With one quick motion, Trent snapped the gun out of his hand so quickly the gang member gasped in shock.

Chloe grinned. Yeah, there was nothing quite like seeing Trent in fighter mode. Too bad she couldn't afford the time to stick around and watch. She tumbled from the stuffed animals. Toys cascaded across the floor. She allowed herself just one more glimpse of Trent's strong form now fighting for all their lives against not one but two Gulos. Her fighting style was precise and tactical, based on an understanding of anatomy and physics. But Trent was a blistering force, all power and instinct.

She rolled to the platform and peered under. Four pairs of stunned eyes met hers.

"Come on!" she said. "We've got to get you guys out of here."

"You're Coach's fiancée, right?" The whispered question came from a young man with curly brown hair and a composure that implied this wasn't his first crisis. Under any other circumstances she would've laughed.

"No, I'm a cop." She pulled her badge out and pushed it in front of his face. "You are?"

"Aidan. I'm the center for Third Line."

So, the hockey equivalent of a third-string quarterback then.

"Okay, Aidan. I'm going to crawl around to the other side of this platform, and you four are going to meet me there. We're all going to stay really low and head down the hallway. Once I give the word, you're going to jump to your feet and sprint to the exit as fast as you can. Nice and simple. Got it? Now let's go."

She turned to crawl away but felt a hand grab her ankle. It had to be Lucy's brother, Brandon. Dark hair falling over an angular face, his earnest eyes were deep with worry. "I have to find my sister, miss. She works at the coffee counter."

Being called "miss" grated. She preferred Detective or Officer. But she couldn't begin to imagine how he must be feeling and now was no time to quibble. "You're Brandon, right?"

He nodded. "Brandon. Brandon Butler."

She blinked. Frank Butler's grandson? She vaguely remembered seeing his grandchildren from a distance at their grandmother's funeral. "Your sister's okay. She made it out safely."

"Thank you." He let out a long breath and closed his eyes for a split second as he whispered a prayer. But the anxiety in his face didn't fade. "What about Coach Henri?"

He pronounced the French version of "Henry" like the letter *H* was silent, so it almost sounded like "Enry." Seemed Trent hadn't strayed too far from his real last name on this cover. But as Trent liked to say the best covers always contained a hint of truth.

"Don't worry. Your coach is going to be okay." Now,

to hurry up and get them all out of there before they noticed just how okay he was doing.

Trent was still battling two Gulos at once. He was such a strong fighter he seemed almost invincible, except that she happened to know he'd dislocated his shoulder once or twice in the past. She prayed it wouldn't happen this time, and would come back to assist him once she got the civilians out.

She crawled flat on her stomach around the side of the stage, where the students were already making their way out from under the platform. The second-floor Gulo was nowhere to be seen. She waved a hand at the hockey players and started toward the wall, her body low as she moved across the floor on her forearms. The players followed. They reached the wall and she waved them on, putting herself between the young men and the gang members, praying the Gulos wouldn't see them.

The sport center's main hallway lay long and empty ahead of them in a maze of destruction and broken glass. The doors shone at the end as headlights blazed in the darkened parking lot, sending a blinding white glow against the glass, punctuated by dashes of moving red and blue. Emergency services had arrived.

Gunfire and vile shouts sounded from above. A huge decorative snowflake crashed to the floor ahead of them and shattered. They'd been spotted.

"Run!" She leaped to her feet and ran forward, pausing just long enough to make sure each and every member of the team had made it to their feet and was moving. Bullets rang behind her. The youths sprinted down the hallway. Chloe ran behind them, taking up the rear and urging the boys on.

The doors in front of them opened. Cops leaned in, reaching out for them. The young men ran through, guided by police. One by one they disappeared into the parking lot. *Thank You, God!* They were going to make it. Every single civilian Trent had been protecting was going to be okay.

Footsteps pounded down the hall behind her as the last player tumbled through the door. A hand grabbed her neck and yanked her backward so suddenly she felt her feet slip out from under her. A plastic mask pressed against her cheek. A rough voice barked past her ear, "Stay back! This pretty little thing is mine!"

The cops stepped back. The door closed. For one quick moment her eyes searched the hallway behind her. Two Gulos lay on the floor where Trent had been fighting just moments before. Trent was gone. Her body was pulled backward into an office. She looked up into the cold, plastic stare of an old-fashioned goalie mask.

She'd been taken hostage and Trent had left her to fight for her life alone.

Trent watched through the eyeholes of the vintage goalie mask as fear filled Chloe's face. A gasp slipped through her lips. He winced. Didn't she know it was him? Didn't she understand that he just needed to grab one quick moment to tell her what she needed to know about his undercover investigation before she ran into a mob of local cops? The security cameras in the center might be so bad they were practically nonexistent, but that didn't mean he wanted a phalanx of officers—let alone Butler—seeing the local hockey coach yanking a provincial detective away for a private chat.

"Hey, it's okay." He let go of her body and reached up to pull his mask off. He didn't get the opportunity. Chloe's strikes came hard and fast, beating him around the head and sending the mask spinning until he could barely see through the eyeholes. "Chloe! Stop! It's me—"

A strong, precise and determined kick caught him in the gut and sent him flying back against the wall. She'd knocked the air right out of his lungs. He could barely make himself heard in this stupid mask. Or she was so determined to fight she wasn't even listening.

Her fists flew toward him again. Enough! He could hardly get this stupid mask off if she kept attacking him. He ducked her blow, swung her around and pressed her back up against the wall. He braced his forearm across her chest, pinning her, and yanked the mask off his face. "Chloe! Stop! It's me!"

"Trent?" The fear and the fight fell from her face. Her eyes went wide.

They were standing so close his arm was the only thing keeping her chest from touching his, and he could feel her heartbeat radiating through it. For a moment he couldn't tell if she was tempted to slap him or to hug him. He stepped back and raised both hands in front of him before either could happen. "I can't believe you didn't know it was me! Don't you remember when we first worked together undercover, I called you a 'pretty little thing' and then you pretended to be mad at me."

"That wasn't pretend." She blew out a long breath. "Not that I expect you to understand that."

He didn't know what she meant by that, but now was hardly the time for arguments. "Are there any casualties?"

"Not that I know of," she said. "There are two college students in the upstairs exercise room—a young woman named Poppy and a hockey player from Haliburton named Johnny. They're on the phone with 9-1-1 and barricaded themselves in. I also helped Brandon's sister, Lucy, escape. She told me the security guard had gotten out, too."

"And hostiles?" he asked. "I disarmed three."

"I only saw three, too." She touched her right sweatshirt pocket with the back of her hand, like she was checking to make sure something was still there. "Look, I don't know what you're playing at, Henry, but you have exactly sixty seconds to explain what's going on. Because now, thanks to you, there's probably a whole parking lot full of cops thinking that one of their own is being held hostage by a goof in a goalie mask."

A goof?

"What are you even doing here?" he asked. Trust Chloe to barge into the middle of his undercover investigation and start demanding answers. "You just happened to be hanging out in a random, small-town sports center when gang violence broke out?"

"I've been popping by here to work out," she said, without meeting his eyes. "I have the week off work, and I own a house in the country about half an hour from here. This is the closest gym that has a pool and equipment room."

He didn't doubt she was telling the truth. The Chloe he knew would never lie to him, and it wasn't unheard of for people in rural parts of Ontario to drive even farther for a grocery store or bank. Other college athletes and teams came from all over the area to use the facilities and rink. But, he also knew her well enough to know that there was more to it than just that. Fine, if she wanted to keep things to herself, so could he. His eyes traced down her slender throat to the lanyard she wore with her detective's badge.

"You identified yourself as a cop," he said.

"Of course I did. I had to rescue multiple people, report a crime in progress to the authorities and fight for my life against a Gulo gang member. So, yeah, I was going to pull on everything I could to get through." Her arms crossed over her badge. "And your minute is down to thirty seconds."

He let out a long breath and ran one hand through his hair. It was a lot shaggier than he liked, not to mention a bit of white had started to creep in at the temples right before he'd turned thirty-six. Then he ran his hand over his beard. That had taken some getting used to, too.

"I'm undercover—"

"I got that. You're Coach Henri."

"And a teacher at Trillium College," he said. "And you're here because of the payara investigation, aren't you?"

"Not officially," she said. "But I won't deny I've been very curious. Gossip's running pretty thick that Butler's botched the investigation so badly so far that some people think he's corrupt." Her tone implied she wasn't one of them. He wasn't sure what Butler had done to earn such loyalty from her.

"And you've been hanging out here because you thought he could use your help?"

Something flashed in the depths of her eyes. "Well, I'm guessing you think you could, too, considering you kept calling me."

"Maybe," he said. He crossed his arms, too. "I'm undercover, trying to find who's been making payara. Yes, I wanted your input. But, no, that doesn't mean I wanted you to barge in and snoop around. All I wanted was to go out for a simple coffee—"

"Because you're so good at showing up for coffee."

Yikes! She was still upset about that? Yes, he knew last time they'd spoken, months ago, he'd made plans to meet up with her at a diner. But then he'd gotten a new, immediate assignment and it had seemed easier just to leave than to go through the messiness of explaining he didn't know when he'd be able to talk to her again. Looks like he'd made the wrong decision.

"I apologize for that. Standing you up was a mistake." Asking her out in the first place had been an even bigger one. What had he been thinking? A woman like her was way out of his league, and the nature of his work made it all but impossible to form real relationships. "I could give you a long explanation, but it would all come down to the fact that I had a new case to start and had to disappear. If you want a longer explanation it will have to wait for another time. You're a cop. I'm a cop. All that matters now is dealing with the mess we're in."

She didn't answer, but she also didn't argue. He took that as a signal to keep going.

"Yes, a baggie of payara was found in the hockey team locker room garbage can a few months ago," he went on, talking as quickly as he could. "It contained thousands of dollars' worth of pills. It's like nothing our drug guys have ever seen before. And, as you know, a drug can't be properly banned until its exact chemical compounds are analyzed and made illegal, which means anyone arrested for dealing it is at risk of bouncing. I'm told it feels like a superhigh burst of adrenaline and endorphins without a crash afterward, which makes it popular with students and athletes. Also makes people aggressive, highly suggestible and wrecks their impulse control."

"So, it's your job to figure out how the drugs ended up in a small little town like Bobcaygeon?" she asked.

"The opposite. Bobcaygeon is the source. We've never busted anyone with more than a few pills on them. So a great, big baggie-full turning up in a sports center locker room is the biggest break we've had in the case. We suspect one of the third-line players you rescued left it there. The assistant coach had them skating laps the night the drugs were found. There was no payara in the locker room when they walked into it and thousands of dollars of it in a baggie in the garbage can when they walked out—"

"By who?" she interjected.

"I don't know," he admitted. And he should. He'd

cracked much harder cases in much shorter periods of time. "Either nobody knows but the one guy who threw it there, or the others have chosen to keep it secret to protect each other. I don't know which. Police apparently couldn't get them to crack, so I went in undercover to try to build a relationship with them."

Light dawned in her eyes. "No wonder people think Butler is corrupt if there're only four possible leads and one of them is his grandson Brandon."

He almost smiled. This was the Chloe he'd missed. The one whose brain was so quick and sharp he could almost feel it sharpening his. "I've spent a lot of time with Third Line and none of them strike me as criminal material. Not to mention I still have no idea where in town the drug lab is or who's making the drugs."

"Why do I get the impression this is urgent?" she asked.

"One way or the other, my cover job finishes after Christmas. I'm supposed to start a much larger gang-related investigation in the new year."

"Wow. Ticktock." Chloe slid past him, filling his senses with lavender and wood smoke. She always smelled far better than any cop had business smelling. "So, what's the plan?"

"The fact that everyone knows you're a cop is going to complicate matters if we're seen together." He ran his hand over the back of his neck. Further complicating matters was the fact that he had a picture of them together, smiling and hugging like the happy couple they sometimes pretended to be, displayed prominently on the desk in his office at Trillium. Fictional relationship ties were an important addition to an undercover persona, and he'd happened to still have the photo around from an undercover case they'd worked together. Thankfully she didn't know about that. "You go out there and do what you do. I'll wait a few minutes and come out after you. Then hopefully we can meet up later and talk further."

A smile curled at the corner of her lips. "And what exactly do I do?"

"You know. You say the right things. You make everything work the way it's supposed to. You fix things." He didn't know how to explain it, let alone define it. She was just smart about seeing the bigger picture stuff. He tended to fight in the moment.

"And how do you expect me to explain to the police how a mild-mannered teacher and hockey coach took out three Gulos?" she asked.

"One has a dislocated shoulder and mild concussion from trying to throw a bad punch that didn't land quite where he expected."

"You should be thankful you didn't dislocate your shoulder again," she said.

Despite himself, Trent chuckled. "Another was accidentally shot by his buddy whose aim was off, and a hockey coach kindly checked his wound and told him to put pressure on it. The third was already pretty badly roughed up in a fight with a brave and beautiful lady cop. All I did was make sure he tripped while running down the stairs after her. They were all very clumsy."

"Real cute, Trent." Her lips pursed and he could tell

she was impressed, despite herself. "But if you ever call me that again, I'm decking you for real."

His face paled as his brain caught up with what his mouth had said. He'd called her beautiful. She had to know she could make a guy's tongue forget how to form words just by walking into a room. But why had he said it? "Sorry."

"Fine. But don't ever let me hear you call me Lady Cop again. It's Detective Brant. Got it?"

"Got it." Relief swept over him. Her hand slid back to her pocket. It was that move people made when trying to check something was still in their pocket, and it was the second time she'd done it. He could feel his detective instincts buzzing at the back of his brain.

"You were right," she said. "I was here working out because I'd heard about the payara and I wanted in on the investigation.

"When I trained under Butler, he was so sharp. I can't begin to imagine why he hasn't solved the payara case yet. But I'm putting my name in for a detective sergeant's job this spring and don't want the fact that I trained under Butler wrecking that for me. Hopefully, I can help clear him. If not, maybe I can confront him in a way that's respectful of his long career.

"Either way, I'm asking you, Trent, cop to cop, to find me an official role on the case. Nothing undercover or in your way. I can chase leads, conduct interviews or review evidence. Whatever you need. Just let's call our bosses and get me officially assigned to assist you from behind the scenes."

He laughed. It was a reflexive, defensive move and

one he immediately regretted. Hadn't she heard him? He was down to his last week before this entire assignment had to end. And now he was supposed to ask for a provincial officer to be assigned to his federal case and find something for her to do? "No. Sorry. I'm not bringing someone else in officially at this stage. I want unofficial advice from you, nothing more."

Chloe took a step back and pulled out a cell phone. "I took this off one of the Gulos."

Trent felt his heart stop. She was holding a drug dealer's cell phone right out in front of his nose, and he needed it. They both knew how easily he could slide his hand around her slender wrist and take it from her, and that if she were a hostile, or a civilian, or someone other than Chloe Brant, he just might. Instead he watched as her fingers tightened around it.

"You know as well as I do, I'm under no obligation to hand this over to you," she said. "I could log it through the OPP and let you make an official request for the data, which we both know could take a while to go through. After all, I haven't received official confirmation of anything you've told me. All I've got to go on right now is trust. Nothing more—"

There was the crash of glass doors shattering. Loud voices shouted in the hall behind him, announcing police presence. Chloe slid the phone back into her pocket. "I'll find you and we can talk later."

She stepped out into the hallway, her badge held high.

Trent counted slowly backward from a hundred. Then he stepped out into the hallway. A cop stood in front of him. She was young, blonde and wearing a bulletproof vest. She pointed her weapon at Trent. "Hands up! You're under arrest!"

THREE

Trent raised both hands above his head.

"I'm Coach Travis Henri," he said, giving his under-cover name. "I'm the Trillium College hockey coach. Who are you?"

"Constable Nicole Docker." She didn't even blink. "Hands behind your head."

Trent held his tongue and complied, letting her cuff his hands behind his back and then lead him into the main foyer. With each step he fought the urge to re-mind her that she hadn't told him what he was being charged with or informed him of his rights. It was his job to figure out where the drugs were coming from. Incompetent cops weren't his problem. Not unless they were making or selling payara.

"Constable, let him go!" an authoritative voice barked to their right, accompanied by the sharp sound of footsteps. Trent looked up. A tall, uniformed man in his late sixties was striding down the hallway. It was Staff Sergeant Frank Butler. "And get those ridiculous handcuffs off him!"

Trent watched the staff sergeant approach as the female officer removed his cuffs. Butler was an elder by cop standards, with short-cropped white hair, a healthy outdoor tan and the kind of athletic build that looked like he could easily take on men a third of his age and win. But he was jittery, too, with a slight but telltale shake to his limbs that Trent usually associated with people who had something to hide. "It's Coach Henri, from Trillium, right?" he said.

Trent nodded. "That's me."

"I'm Frank Butler, Brandon's grandfather," the staff sergeant said. He stretched out his hand. "I'm sorry, I don't think we've ever been properly introduced."

The handshake was a little too firm and Trent couldn't help but notice that Constable Nicole Docker had seemingly evaporated.

"It's nice to finally meet you," Trent said. Despite nodding to each other at hockey games, Trent and the staff sergeant had never actually had much of a conversation. That was on purpose. Trent had learned long ago that when he was trying to maintain a cover, the less time he spent talking to local cops the better.

"I apologize for all that." Butler frowned. "I imagine that was your first time in handcuffs. Must've been quite the shock to the system."

Trent laughed. It was a safe, noncommittal response. He'd been handcuffed and arrested more times than he could count. It had usually been as part of his undercover work. But the first couple of times he'd been an out-of-control teen, just on the edge of the Wolfspiders gang's grasp and dealing with the fact that his twelve-year-old sister had been killed when he'd failed to show up to walk her home from school.

"They were under orders to be on the lookout for someone matching your description," Butler continued. "We saw someone in a mask and mistakenly thought it was a threat. But Detective Brant explained that it was all just a silly misunderstanding and that you'd been trying to help. Next time, keep your head down, stay out of trouble and leave matters to the professionals, all right?"

"Understood," Trent said. He wondered if there was a reason Butler was pushing him away from the case, beside the fact that he presumed he was a civilian. "Brandon and the other third-line players got out okay?"

"They did, thankfully," Butler said. "Thank you for telling them to hide."

"You must've been worried sick," Trent said.

"To be honest, I had no idea he was even in there until he came running out the front door. The young men are saying you stayed behind to fight the gang members?"

"Well, they jumped me, so I fought them off the best I could." Trent chuckled self-consciously. "Guess my inner hockey brawler came out. I was a bit of a fighter in my youth. Not the kind of stuff I'd ever tolerate from my players, but handy in a situation like that. My dad always said I was all instinct and no common sense. Told me I'd get myself killed one day."

That was more truth than he liked admitting, but he'd always believed truth made the best cover. His dad was a farmer who hadn't quite known how to handle his second eldest son. What he'd actually told him, more times than Trent could count, was that if he didn't learn to take a breath instead of flying off the handle, he'd get himself or somebody else killed. Then, a teenaged Trent would come within an inch of shouting back, "You mean like I killed my sister?" before running off and doing something stupid like punching a hole in the barn wall.

He shook off the ugly memory.

"One of the masked men asked me if I knew where he could score some drugs," Trent added. "The name sounded a bit like 'pariah' or 'piranha.' But, like I told him, I honestly have no idea what that stuff is made of, let alone where to get it."

"Just remember to leave things like that to the police in the future," Butler said again. "The last thing we need is civilians running around the place trying to be heroes. Now, if you can please head outside, somebody will take your statement."

Dismissed, Trent walked outside. Cold, wet air hit him like a wave. The sun would be rising soon, but snow was now pelting down in sheets. Emergency vehicles and camera crews filled the parking lot. People huddled together in pockets around a tall fir tree decked in Christmas lights. They were so shrouded by winter gear and emergency blankets he could barely tell who was who. More specifically, he couldn't see Chloe anywhere.

A slender hand came out of nowhere, grabbing him firmly by the arm and pulling him under an overhang. He blinked. Chloe had pulled the furry hood of a jacket up over her head. It framed her face perfectly and made her look years younger. Wisps of red hair flew around her face. The overall effect was kind of adorable.

"You infuriate me, Henry," Chloe said. "You really do. You've been calling me for days and you didn't once think to mention what you were calling me about? Why were you even calling me if you didn't want me involved with this investigation?"

He was beginning to think it might actually have been because he'd missed her.

"I told you," he said. "I'm undercover at your old college. Bobcaygeon is your hometown. You worked with Butler and you live half an hour from here."

"Trillium is not my college." She frowned. "It's just a community college I happened to go to, before getting into the police academy. Bobcaygeon is not my hometown and owning a house somewhere I crash at between cases isn't the same as living there."

Well, obviously that bothered her. But he had no idea why. "So, you're not from here, then?"

"I thought you knew me better than that, Cop Boy. I'm not from anywhere."

"Cop Boy? I can't call you Lady Cop, but you can call me Cop Boy?" Despite himself, she'd just made him laugh. Yeah, he had missed her. He'd missed this. The light teasing. The verbal sparring. The sense that he always had to be on his toes around her. "How can you possibly be from nowhere? Everyone's from somewhere."

"Not me. My little sister, Olivia, and I grew up in the back of a station wagon, squished between suitcases. I don't know if our dad's intentionally a con artist, or just the kind of man who's really good at temporarily hiding the fact that he's a jerk and convincing people he's good at things he's not. But he has the kind of attitude problem that makes him think that nobody is ever treating him well enough. His charm makes him great at landing jobs. But his sense of entitlement makes him terrible at keeping them.

"So we'd land somewhere new, get settled in, live there for a few months, and then he'd get into an argument with someone and back into the station wagon we'd go. Bobcaygeon happened to be where I was for the last three months of high school and I entered Trillium because moving twice in grade twelve had killed my ability to get a student loan for university. That doesn't mean I belonged here."

That had been a defensive monologue he hadn't expected. What had gotten under her skin? "Then why do you own a house half an hour from here?"

"When my mother finally decided she'd had enough of my father, she had no bank account of her own and a divorce lawyer wasn't much help in taking half of my father's nothing. She begged me to cosign on a mortgage for her. So I did. I was twenty-two." She crossed her arms. "A few years ago, she decided she wanted to move into a retirement building in Southern Ontario, so I took over the mortgage. I tend to rent a place wherever I'm working, so I just use it as a place to crash and leave my stuff. I'm sure you know exactly what I'm talking about and expect you're in the same boat."

The huge warm Henry family farmhouse where he'd be celebrating Christmas dinner swept into his mind unbidden. He could almost feel the warmth of the fire in the living room, smell the hay in the barn and hear the rattle of cutlery and the babble of voices in the dining room as his parents and three brothers passed dishes around. No, he knew exactly what it was like to be from somewhere. He also knew what it was like to feel like he didn't really belong there. He blinked and the thought was gone, replaced with the pale light, snow and Chloe's eyes on his face.

"I hear you," he said, waiting for his mind to catch up with his words. "But, like I told you, I'm on borrowed time. My cover was never supposed to drag out this long and is now nearing its expiration date. I have to figure out who's making the stuff. That means finding who's selling it, and I've spent three months completely failing to make the kind of inroads I need to with these students."

"Hey, Officer Brant!" a female voice shouted. They turned. It was Poppy, an outspoken and dark-haired student he vaguely knew from one of his classes. She was running across the parking lot, dragging Hodge, one of his third-line players, after her.

"Poppy!" A smile filled Chloe's face. "Glad to see you got out okay."

"Yeah. Johnny and I piled some weights up against the door, and we stayed low until the police came for us." She propelled Hodge forward.

Trent couldn't help but notice that the young man wasn't exactly smiling. Jeremy Hodgekins, better known as "Hodge," was a giant, with a sturdy six-foot-three frame and a bright future, if he could figure out how to stay out of trouble long enough to make it through college. As far as Trent knew, he was the only member of Third Line to ever find himself in the back of a police cruiser, but only for throwing punches and nothing that had earned him more than a warning. "This is Hodge."

"Hey," the young man said. "Thanks for your help."

"No problem," Chloe said. "It was a team effort. Your coach really saved our lives and had our backs."

Hodge didn't look convinced.

See, this was Trent's problem. He could walk into any dangerous and dingy bar in the country and demand immediate respect because people knew in a glance what he was capable of. But these students? He'd never give them a reason to fear him and they'd never have a reason to trust him. Poppy whispered something in Hodge's ear. He ran his eyes over Chloe.

"Yeah, maybe," Hodge said. He nodded to Trent. "That's your fiancée, right? The one whose picture you showed us. Aidan thinks so, anyway. Why didn't you tell us you were marrying a cop?"

Heat rose to the back of Trent's neck. He forced a grin on his face and didn't meet Chloe's eye.

"Well, like I told you guys, she works in northern Ontario," Trent said. "But she came through when I needed her."

Hodge nodded like that was enough of an explanation. The students wandered back into the crowd. Trent turned to Chloe. "I can explain—"

"You don't need to," Chloe said quickly. "You're undercover. You used an old picture of me as a prop for your cover identity. It makes perfect sense."

Did it? There was something he couldn't quite place in her tone. Then again, something about being this close to Chloe threw his radar off.

"I just hope the fact that they now know I'm a cop won't hurt your cover," she added.

So did he. He took a deep breath and prayed. *Lord, You've been the one consistent presence through everyone I've ever been or pretended to be. I asked You for help. Is Chloe showing up Your answer?*

"We can work with it," he said. "I need that cell phone, and I could honestly use a second brain on this case. I used that old fake-engagement picture of us taken on the gondola at Blue Mountain to bolster my cover. It was an impulse more than a grand plan, but now that you're here, we can use it to our advantage.

"You'll go undercover for one day as my fiancée. Tomorrow's the twenty-third and the last day of school before the holidays. It's the last hockey game before Christmas, too. I'll take you to the college with me, then we can do the team dinner and you can come to the game. Maybe you'll spot something I've missed. Coach Henri is a big softy, so you'll probably want to play your cover as sweet, cute and kind of gushing. It's not ideal, but it's the only option I can think of and I'm not up for complications right now. So, how about it, Detective? You willing to pretend to be crazily into me in exchange for an official assist on this case?"

Her lips parted. A look floated in her eyes that was so raw the only word he could think to describe it was *personal*. She looked at him like they weren't just two cops—one provincial and one federal—who sometimes

worked together on joint assignments. No, she was looking at him like they were close friends or even former
sweethearts, and like he'd once done something to hurt
her. Then she blinked. The look was gone. "Thanks,
but no. I appreciate why you used my picture for your
cover. But I'm not looking to go undercover with you
like that again."

What? He thought she'd wanted in on this case. All
she had to do was to pretend to be in a relationship with
him for a day.

"I know it's not ideal. But my cover is already set
and there's only so much I can change at this point.
Plus, we've pretended to be a couple before. We play
those roles well."

Maybe even a little too well. There'd been a moment
at the end of the last case where he'd almost wished he'd
had an excuse to drag it out a little longer, which is what
had led to him asking her out for coffee. "It will only be
for a day. Just one day. After that, you'll take the ring
off your finger again and we'll go our separate ways."

But Chloe was still shaking her head. Then she
reached into her pocket, pulled out the cell phone and
pressed it into his hand. "Here. Take it. I'm off duty and
you identified yourself as the lead officer on the scene.
If you need me to write a report about what happened
tonight, get someone to contact my superior officer."

This was unbelievable. The Chloe he knew was te-
nacious. But here she was just handing him her only
leverage and leaving. "But I thought you wanted to be
in on this case!"

"So did I." Her hand brushed his shoulder, sending

odd and unexpected shivers up his spine. "But I think I was wrong. Take care of yourself, Trent. I really hope this works out well for you."

His mouth opened but he couldn't think of any words to fill it. Chloe was walking away and he didn't know what to say or how to stop her. The phone was in his possession. He'd just won the argument. So why did it feel like he'd just lost something much more important than that?

Chloe's cell rang. Headlights shone against her living room window, filling it with a brief flash of light. Then the glass went dark again. She sat up and looked out. Snow beat against the pane. Wind shook the glass. The clock read a quarter to seven in the morning. She picked up her cell and glanced at it to see a missed a call from a blocked number. It had to be Trent. But he was the last person she wanted to talk to right now. It was bad enough she'd just turned down the opportunity to work on the payara case and mitigate the damage an investigation into Butler could do to her career, the last thing she wanted was to try to explain to him why.

He'd asked her to pretend she had feelings for him.

Chloe sighed and lay back on the couch. She'd been wired after leaving the sports center. She hadn't spotted Butler at all after walking away from Trent, so she hadn't had the opportunity to really talk to him except for the few rushed words they'd exchanged in the moments after she'd first run out the sports center. The brief conversation she'd had at the scene with a rookie female officer named Nicole Docker hadn't told her much of anything. So she'd gone for a drive, then shopping and finally a long walk through the woods surrounding her rural, country house.

All the while she'd felt the problem of Trent and the payara investigation moving through her mind like the tumblers of a lock she couldn't quite open. When she'd told him she wanted in on the investigation, she'd envisioned something strictly professional—something that wouldn't involve staring longingly into his eyes while he pretended he had feelings for her.

But something about standing there with him in the early morning light as he'd asked her to act like she was crazy about him had sent her heart pounding like she was cresting the top of a roller coaster without knowing how big the drop was on the other side. She was done with chaos and the men who caused it. Working undercover with Trent was like eating a six-scoop ice-cream sundae with whipped cream, bananas, caramel and chocolate drizzle. It was an incredible thrill, which made her feel like she was working at the very top of her game. That was, until he'd left her sitting alone in a coffee shop wondering how she'd fooled herself into thinking he actually cared.

Her fake engagement ring from their last undercover mission lay on the coffee table. She'd dug it out of her jewelry box when she'd gotten home and wasn't quite sure why she'd bothered keeping it, considering it was probably only worth a few dollars and she'd never be able to wear it without thinking of Trent. She picked it up and twirled it around in her fingers. It was a heavy, solid ring inlaid with intricate strands of imitation diamonds and emeralds. It felt expensive. Not that she believed for a moment it was anything more than a good piece of costume jewelry. When Trent had given it to her at the start of their last assignment, he told her he'd fished it out of a mud puddle at a truck stop.

Headlights moved past her window for a second time. She looked out. It was a dark pickup. Was it the same driver passing twice or just a coincidence? Her cell phone buzzed again, and this time her sister's contact picture flashed on the screen. She dropped the ring and answered it. "Olivia! Hi!"

"Chloe!" Her sister's voice was breathless, almost flustered. "Hi! I hope this isn't too early. Abby's been teething. Molars, I think. So time has lost all meaning."

"No problem. Now is perfect." Besides, she was thankful to have something to replace the dangerously attractive picture of Trent that still floated at the edges of her mind. Instead she thought about Olivia. Five years younger and almost a foot shorter, both Olivia and her one-year-old Abigail had the same startling green eyes and red hair that Chloe had. A journalist, Olivia lived with her bodyguard husband, Daniel, two hours away. "Everything okay?"

"You asked me to let you know if I heard anything about Staff Sergeant Butler's OPP division in Bobcaygeon. There was a major gang shooting there yesterday—"

"I know." Chloe cut her off. "I was there. I'm sorry. I should've told you."

Olivia's voice froze midstream as it switched tone between journalist and sister. "Are you okay?"

"I'm fine," Chloe said. "I'm sorry I didn't call you earlier. Can we talk off the record?"

"Okay. But just so you know, the newspaper will be launching a major investigation into rumors that Butler botched a drug investigation. We'll be starting it the first week of January. We've been hearing it from several sources and this gang violence has given us a pretty strong hook."

"Got it." Chloe blew out a long breath. *Torchlight News* would be thorough and fair. And Chloe could no more ask Olivia not to run a news story than Olivia could ask her not to investigate a crime. "I saw Trent Henry."

"Wow," Olivia said. "And?"

"He asked me to help him out on an undercover case."

"You said yes, didn't you?" Olivia sighed. "Clo, you've got a rescue complex."

"No, I don't." True, there'd been a time when a simple phone call from her sister would be enough to make her drop everything and rush to help her, because her sister wasn't as strong and steady as she was. But Olivia had Daniel now, plus a whole team of bodyguards who worked for him.

"So says the woman trying to save her former training officer's career," Olivia countered.

"That's different. Butler trained me. I owe him some loyalty for that. Not to mention it won't exactly be great for my career if he's thrown under the bus."

Although seeing how little faith Trent apparently had in Butler was worrying.

"I told Trent no. I don't need the headache of Trent Henry right now. I mean, I'd like in on the specific investigation. I can't go into any details on what it's about, obviously. It would be great for helping me land that promotion. But Trent said it would mean posing as his fiancée and when he said that something inside me just balked. Something about pretending to be dating Trent wrecks me emotionally every time. Plus, I don't want him thinking he can just sweep into my life, disrupting everything, whenever he thinks he needs me and then just disappear again." She liked order. Trent was chaos. And, if she did have a rescue complex, it was clear Trent didn't want to be rescued.

"But you like him," Olivia said. "And he likes you."

"So? We're not teenagers. I'm not picking a buddy to do a book report with. And even if I was, Trent's the kind of guy who'd ditch class the day the report was due because he suddenly had something else come up."

"You could bring him for Christmas dinner," Olivia said. "It's going to be a big shindig. We're inviting all of Daniel's Ash Security colleagues and their partners. Both Josh and Alex are newlyweds. Zoe's fiancé has two amazing daughters. Abby adores them."

Was her sister even listening to what she was saying? It was like she was having a completely different conversation.

"Trent Henry is the last person I can imagine sitting around a table at Christmas dinner," Chloe said. "He doesn't want a relationship with me. He wants to pretend to have a relationship with me when it suits him, and then walk out of my life without saying goodbye."

She couldn't begin to get her head around why that was so much trouble for her heart. She just knew that it was.

"What do you want?" Olivia pressed.

"A cast-iron heart that he can't even dent," she said. Headlights flickered past her window for a third time. She tossed the blanket off and stood. It was the same truck. "I've got to go. Just pray for me, okay? And I'll see you at Christmas."

"Will do."

The call ended. Chloe shoved her feet into boots and yanked her arms through the sleeves of her jacket. It was probably nothing. But she'd slip through the woods by the road and watch for the truck to drive by again, just in case, and then search the plates.

She opened the door. It flew back instantly, knocking her hard in the chest and throwing her off balance. A large man—huge, bald and shrouded in winter clothes—shoved his way into her living room, kicking the door closed behind him. Her hands rose to protect herself. But it was too late.

He pushed her down onto the couch, tossing her like a rag doll. One hand clenched her throat. The other held a handgun to her cheek.

"I don't know what your game is," the man hissed. "But you took a cell phone off a Gulo yesterday, and you're going to give it to me."

FOUR

She was pinned down helplessly on her own couch, in her own home, watching as a criminal waved a gun before her eyes. *Lord, help me! Please!*

She didn't regret giving Trent the cell phone. It had been the right thing to do. But as she felt the squeeze tighten on her throat, she knew without a doubt that it was a decision she might now die for.

In all the years she'd been on the job, nobody had ever entered her home or breached her sanctuary. No matter how vile and terrible the investigation, she'd always been able to draw a firm line behind it and walk away. Now the danger had followed her home.

He tightened his grip on her throat. "I'll ask you again. Where is that cell phone?"

"I gave it to a police officer." Her voice rasped. If only she could get some leverage, she might be able to defend herself. But she was on her back and sinking deep into the cushions, her legs bent awkwardly beneath her and the weight of her attacker on top of her.

"What police officer?" His voice was a deep snarl.

His eyes were two bloodshot circles of black. "Give me a name!"

She couldn't. She couldn't risk Trent's cover. Tears filled her eyes. She was about to be killed—or worse—to protect Trent, unless she found a way out.

Come on, Chloe. Focus! Don't let fear win! Her rational brain spun. The face was that of a stranger and the fact that he wasn't wearing a mask meant he probably wasn't planning on leaving her alive. The bulging muscles implied steroid use. He was bald and a tattoo on his neck looked like some kind of spider's web made of fangs. Her words came out staccato through shallow gasps. "One of the cops…who was at the sports center… He was plainclothes… I didn't see a badge…"

Vile swear words flowed from his lips. The barrel of the gun dug into the soft flesh under her chin, tilting her head all the way back. His hand moved from her neck to his pocket. He pulled out a pair of zip-tie handcuffs.

She grabbed the gun with both hands and yanked it high above her head while she arched, freeing her legs and pulling them into her chest. Then she kicked up hard with both feet, sending him flying forward, over her head and off the end of the couch, wrenching the gun from his hand as he went. He hit the floor head-first, with a thud so loud the room seemed to shake. She leaped up and spun around, weapon at the ready. "Don't move. Stay down."

He lunged at her. She pulled the trigger. The gun jammed. Again, her fingers squeezed the trigger. Another futile click, followed by a roar as the brute's body launched into hers. He tossed her backward again.

She hit the corner of the coffee table. The gun fell from her hand and pain shot through her spine. *Lord, please give me strength.* She leveled a strong blow to his jaw. He stumbled back.

She turned and ran for the door, burst outside and into the deep gray of an early winter morning. Bitter wind whipped against her. Her skin stung with the threat of frostbite.

There was a truck parked on the road. She looked up. Trent was sauntering up the gravel driveway, toward her, a takeout coffee cup in each hand.

"Trent!" she gasped.

"Chloe?" His clear blue eyes met hers and worry filled their depths. In a quick, almost seamless motion, he set the coffee cups down and ran for her, and it took all the strength left in her body not to crumple into his outstretched arms. "Tell me."

"There's a man…in my house… He wants the cell phone…"

"You're hurt." Trent's fingers gingerly brushed along the side of her throat.

Something she'd never seen before pooled in the depths of his eyes. Something protective. Something comforting.

"He choked you."

"He tried to strangle me." Her limbs were shaking. She wanted to fall into the strength of Trent's arms and let him hold her. Instead she pushed him. "I'm okay. Go! Stop him!"

"Wait in my truck." He pushed a set of car keys into her hand. "Just to be safe. It's already warmed up and, unlike your car, isn't buried in snow. Stay there. Stay safe." Trent's hand touched her shoulder for one fleeting moment. Then he pelted toward the house.

Her limbs shook from the cold and from shock. She picked up the closest coffee cup and took a sip. It was thick with both cream and sugar, neither of which she usually took. But it was soothing in her throat and she was thankful for that. This was all wrong. Danger wasn't supposed to follow her home. Trent wasn't supposed to show up to her rescue. For the first time, since she'd lived under her father's roof she didn't feel in control of her life. Instead, she felt like a player in somebody else's story, and the thought of that tightened her throat so painfully she could almost feel the hands of the intruder clenched around them again.

An engine roared. A snowmobile shot out from behind the house and disappeared into the forest.

Her attacker had gotten away.

Trent stood in Chloe's living room. Signs of a struggle surrounded him on all sides. The coffee table was cracked. Shelves were knocked over. Frustration burned at the back of his throat. Chloe's attacker had burst out of the house and gone to his snowmobile so quickly that Trent had never even gotten a glimpse of his face. He could've gone after him. He could've leaped into his truck, raced down the back roads, cut him off, run him into a ditch and yanked him from the snowmobile.

Instead, seeing the ugly red marks on her pale skin had stalled something in his brain and kept him from leaving Chloe. His sister had been strangled to death when she'd been twelve and he was thirteen, because he'd made her walk home from school alone. And while he'd gotten so adept at his job that he'd long stopped viewing strangulation victims as different from any other, with Chloe it was different. Somehow everything with Chloe had always been different.

A floorboard creaked behind him. He spun. It was Chloe. She was standing in the open doorway of her home with the two coffee cups in her hand.

"Stand back," he said. "I've done a preliminary scan and there doesn't seem to be a second attacker, but it's probably safer if you wait in the truck until I'm absolutely sure."

"This is my house." Chloe stepped over the threshold into the living room and set the coffee cups down on the dining table. Her eyes scanned the room and something in him ached. There was a look in them. It was jaded—sadness, mixed with bitter resignation—as if this wasn't the first time she'd seen her home in disarray. He'd seen a lot of different looks in her eyes, most often focus and determination. But he'd never seen this one before. It was the look of seeing an old enemy return wearing a new face. "So, he's gone?"

"From as far as I can tell. What did he look like?"

"Huge." She hugged herself. "Bald, with bloodshot eyes, a wide nose and bulging muscles. He wore gloves, so we won't be able to pull prints, and he didn't touch anything we could use to get DNA. There was an unusual spiderweb tattoo on his neck. It was like it was made of teeth."

Royd from the Wolfspiders? No, it couldn't be.

There had to be dozens of other men who matched that description besides the former high school friend who'd tried to lure Trent into a life of gang crime when he'd been a teenaged ball of pain and anger. Royd and Royd's sister, Savannah, were like echoes from an ugly past that Trent desperately wished he could forget. Instead, he'd found himself revisiting that old version of himself, time and again, because convincing gang members to trust him was vital to his undercover work, and that meant letting them think he'd never changed.

Lord, You know how much I hate it when my undercover work takes me back to the parts of my past that I'm desperate to forget. Please, help me one day shut down the Wolfspiders for good. Please set me free from my past.

"Are you okay?" Chloe said. "You look like you're about to faint."

"I never faint," he said. He also wasn't about to start opening up ugly chapters of his life and sharing them with her. "It sounds like a Wolfspiders' tattoo. I wouldn't want to guess which particular gang member it is, because there are dozens of them. But it means we've potentially got two different gangs after the payara."

As if the stakes weren't already high enough.

"How would a Wolfspider know that I had a Gulo's phone?" she asked.

"I honestly have no idea," he said. "Everything the Wolfspiders do is coordinated through their leader. He owns a barbecue restaurant near Huntsville that basically acts as a cover. His real name is Stephen Point, but everybody calls him Uncle. The real question is why Uncle told someone to break into your home to retrieve it."

Trent had been waiting more years than he liked admitting to take Uncle down. But the old man kept his hands clean by authorizing crimes and never committing them himself, which had left the crime lord and Trent in an odd cat-and-mouse standoff, where neither risked tipping his hand enough to try to destroy the other. Trent had spent years biding his time, collecting evidence, coordinating arrests of lower level Wolfspiders in ways that didn't lead back to him. One day, Uncle would slip up, commit a crime and get caught red-handed. That day Trent would be waiting. "Walk me through what happened. Take it from the top."

"I saw headlights pass outside my window three times and got up to investigate. I'm guessing now that was you?" she asked. He nodded. She sat on the very edge of the couch, and he noticed the thick smears of mud on the cushions from where someone in boots had climbed on it. "When I opened the door, he forced his way in, grabbed my throat, pushed himself on top of me and demanded I tell him where the phone was."

"You told him I had it, right?" he asked.

"Of course not!" She tossed her hair defiantly. He'd almost never seen it loose. But now it rose and fell in a big swoop around her shoulders, hiding the stark imprint bruises of a thumb and fingers on her neck. "I told him the bare minimum without lying. I told him that I'd given it to a cop at the sports center."

"But he choked you!" Something rose hot and protective at the back of his neck. Why was he arguing with her? She was a cop. She'd done her job. She'd protected the cover of a fellow officer. But someone had tried to strangle her and it was because of him! "He could've killed you!"

"You think I don't know that? I'm a detective with the Special Victims Unit, Trent. Strangulation is pretty much one of the most common ways men attack women in this province. I've had more calls about that type of attack than any other."

Yeah, he knew that. Of course he did. He knew her undercover work usually involved rescuing women and girls from violence, trafficking and other situations so desperate and vile they made his chest ache. He could also rattle off crime stats almost as well as she could. But knowing it in his brain was different from feeling the visceral gut punch of seeing what someone from his former gang had done to Chloe's neck.

"You should have told him that I had it!" He heard his own voice rise.

"Why?" Her voice rose, too. "Because you think that would've stopped him from hurting me? I'd never give up your cover!"

"I know! Chloe, I know what kind of cop you are. I know you'd have let some criminal kill you to protect me. Just like I would for you. But I still wish you'd just told him I had it!"

"Why?" Frustration curled at her lips. "Give me one good reason why I should've thrown your life to the wolves to save mine?"

He couldn't. His heart was pounding in his chest. He was standing there arguing that she should've risked his life and wrecked his current cover, not to mention potentially cutting the knees out from his huge up-coming assignment at a remote diamond mine that he hoped would lead to crippling the Wolfspiders, Gulos and countless other gang operations. He was arguing that she should've wrecked all that for him to save her-self. He didn't know why. He closed his eyes. *What's wrong with me? Why am I acting this way?*

Suddenly he saw himself as a different type of man. He pictured himself crossing the floor, gently brushing his fingers along her delicate skin and softly telling her how very sorry he was that this had happened to her. He imagined his fingers brushing tenderly along her bruised skin and wiping away the tears of fear he could see forming in the corner of her eyes. He saw his lips finding hers and kissing her with a kiss that promised protection. It was the kind of kiss he'd never imagined giving anyone before. Yet he could see it in his mind as clearly as a memory.

"Chloe, I'm sorry he hurt you." Trent opened his eyes. His hands reached out toward her and he wasn't even sure what they were reaching out to do.

"It's okay." She shrugged without really looking at him. Then she picked up one of the coffee cups and took a sip. "At least you knew to be here."

He pulled his arms back. Is that what she thought? That he'd had some heroic inkling she was in danger? No. If anything it was his fault she had seen headlights and opened the door.

"I never dreamed this would happen," he said. "I just dropped by to tell you that when I sent the phone to the tech unit, I made sure you were listed on the report as the officer who'd retrieved it."

He'd decided to tell her that in person, with coffee, because something had seemed off about how they'd parted ways yesterday and he hadn't been able to get her out of his mind. Then he'd driven past her house three times because he'd doubted his decision. He walked over to the table, picked up the full cup and drank. He grimaced. It was black. "I think you drank my coffee. This one is yours."

"Are you sure?" she asked.

"Of course I'm sure." He set the cup down. "I take sugar and cream, you don't."

"You remembered." She stood there a moment, holding the mostly empty cup that had contained his coffee.

"It's hard to forget a coffee order as boring as yours," he said. "You know, they make lots of different interesting coffees these days, with all kinds of milks and weird sugary syrups. You don't have to deprive yourself."

He was trying to be funny. But she frowned and then disappeared into the kitchen, and immediately he regretted saying something that flippant. The truth was he would've remembered her coffee order no matter how complicated it was. She reappeared with a tray, containing two types of milk and three types of sugar. His eyebrow rose as he reached for the plain, white, granular stuff.

"I take it with maple syrup when I'm at home," she said. "I have six different types of coffee in the freezer, and my sister bought me a cappuccino maker last year. But when someone else is pouring it for me, I like to keep it simple. Why cause extra hassle for a barista or waiter by requesting three sugars added to the cup before the coffee is poured and two and a half creams added after?"

His hand jerked so quickly he spilled sugar on the table. That was his usual coffee order. "Because coffee is a universal conversation starter. It's a way of connecting with people. I can't imagine why someone who faces down killers for a living, like you do, would be worried about inconveniencing a waiter."

Her phone rang loud and insistent. She set the coffee down, picked up her cell and held the screen for him to see. It was a blocked number. "This happened earlier. I thought the call was from you."

He shook his head. She answered the phone, turned the speaker volume to maximum and held it a few inches from her ear so that he could listen in.

"Hello?"

"Hello, Officer Brant?" The caller's voice was female. "I know who's making payara."

FIVE

"Yes, this is Detective Brant," Chloe said. Trent felt her reach out, grab his hand and pull him to her side. She led him to the couch and they sat. "Who's this?"

There was a pause. "You can call me Trilly."

Chloe waved her hand toward the pen and pad of paper on the floor. "Nice to meet you, Trilly. Have we met before?"

"No, I don't think so," the voice said.

He grabbed the pad and pushed it into her hands.

Chloe wrote quickly. *Trilly is the Trillium College mascot, right?*

He nodded. Trilly was a cartoon flower with three petals and huge eyes who appeared on things like notice boards.

"Well, I'm happy to help and listen to anything you want to tell me," Chloe said.

There was a long pause on the other end. Chloe waited. Good interrogation was all about knowing when to wait for the other person to talk.

He wrote, *Any guess who she really is?*

She shook her head. *Met three women yesterday. Poppy, Lucy and Nicole.*

He took the pen and wrote, *Nicole tried to arrest me.*

Chloe rolled her eyes.

"You said you were calling about payara?" she prompted.

"Yeah," Trilly said. "It's a drug. They're pills. They're yellowy-orange and make your brain go really fast. Like adrenaline but with no crash."

Not a bad description, but Trent noticed she'd left off the negative side effects like aggression and suggestibility.

"Do you know who's making them?" Chloe asked.

"I do. But I need to make a deal or something. If I give you information, I need some kind of money or plea deal or guarantee that I'm not going to get in trouble for this."

"I want to help," Chloe said. "But I can't help if I don't know what's going on."

"Well, there's a guy involved and it's kind of complicated."

Chloe nodded at Trent as if she'd been expecting it. What was it they said at the academy? Where there were drugs, there was money. Where there was money, there was violence. Where there was violence, there were women in trouble. "Is he your boyfriend?"

"I can't tell you, and he can't know I called you."

This was the part of interrogation he knew well. An informant would get in touch, claiming they wanted to spill information, only to suddenly hold back, make demands or try to force the detective to pry the information out of them. It was infuriating. But Chloe had a knack for it.

Trent's eyes drifted around the room. Something glinted under the broken table. He knelt, felt for it and pulled it out. His heart smacked against his rib cage. It was the ring he'd given her for their fake engagement.

Last winter he'd seen it glittering in a puddle of mud and slush in a truck stop parking lot in northern Ontario. He'd nearly frozen his fingers to the point of numbness trying to fish it out. It had been a gorgeous and valuable thing, lost and forgotten in a terrible place. Immediately, Chloe's face had filled his mind. It was both substantial and beautiful at the same time, which he'd figured was a rare quality in a piece of jewelry, so he'd saved it specifically for her. The fact that their next undercover assignment had required an engagement ring had just been a happy coincidence.

Her hand grabbed his shoulder and squeezed. Chloe was staring down at the ring. He felt his face redden to realize he was literally down on one knee with it in front of her. He sat back up on the couch.

"How about we meet up in person, Trilly?" Chloe said. "Would that help? We could sit down quietly, just you and I, and see if we can work something out."

"Yeah, that could work," Trilly said. "Do you know the hiking path by the gorge? There's a parking lot there."

Trent grabbed Chloe's free hand and squeezed. The parking lot of an isolated gorge in winter? She might as well as be showing up for an actual ambush. He opened his mouth.

Chloe pulled her hand from his grasp. Then she slid a finger over his lips and firmly pushed them shut, as if to say she didn't need his help.

"I don't think that's a good idea," Chloe said. "The roads are terrible. Let's come up with somewhere private enough we can talk alone, but still safe enough it'll be easy for you to leave if you're not happy and want to go."

A bang sounded on the phone. It was like a door opening so quickly it smashed back against a wall. Then he heard footsteps echoing down a hallway.

"Come to the sports center," Trilly said quickly. "Tonight, during the hockey game. I'll meet you in the alley out back, by the garbage cans, during the third period."

"Third period by the garbage cans," Chloe repeated. "I'll be there."

The sound of footsteps grew louder.

"You can't talk to anyone about this and you can't let anybody see you at the game, okay?" Trilly said. "My guy has eyes everywhere. If he sees you around, he'll know you're a detective and get suspicious about why you're hanging around. If I see you around town, anywhere, talking to anyone, I'm bailing."

Chloe closed her eyes for a long moment. A deal like that would be hard to talk her way out of. Trent watched as her lips moved in what looked like silent prayer. Then her eyes opened again and he felt her fingers brush against his skin as she pulled the ring from his grasp.

"Well, I'm going to be at Trillium College, around town and at the hockey game with Coach Henri, today. I'll be everywhere. Your guy, whoever he is, will see me talking to all kinds of people. I might even talk to your guy, considering I don't know who he is and Coach might introduce me."

She slid the ring over the very tip of her third finger on her left hand and let it hover there.

What was she doing? A weird, unsettled feeling filled the pit of his stomach, like she'd grabbed his hand just as she was about to leap off a cliff.

"You can't talk to him," Trilly said. "You can't talk to anyone!"

"It will look a lot more suspicious if I don't." Chloe still didn't meet his eye. Instead, as Trent watched, she slid the ring firmly and smoothly onto her finger. "I'm in town today specifically to spend time with Coach Henri. So I'll be going everywhere he goes and talking to anyone he introduces me to. He's my fiancé."

Chloe held her breath and waited. It was a calculated risk. Refusing to meet Trilly at some remote and unsafe location had been a no-brainer. Only a total amateur would agree to something like that. But announcing she was going to be seen around town with Trent all day talking to whoever she pleased had the potential to be a deal-breaker. Chloe closed her eyes and prayed. Silence dragged on the phone, punctuated by the sound of footsteps coming down a hallway.

"Fine," Trilly said. "Whatever. But you come meet me alone and don't tell anyone about any of this. If I think something's up, I'm bailing."

"Okay." The line went dead. Chloe let out a long breath then set the phone on the table and stood. "I'm guessing you caught most of that? We have an informant who gave us a fake name and claims to know where the payara is coming from."

Trent pushed himself to standing. "You made a snap decision about my cover without consulting me."

"It was your plan!" Her hand waved through the air. The ring felt heavy on her finger. "I thought this is what you'd wanted."

"I thought this is what you didn't want!" he countered.

"I needed to come up with something quickly. Your idea was solid. So I went for it."

He ran his hand over the back of his neck. Why was he being so difficult about this? Sure, she hadn't liked the idea of pretending to be Trent's fiancée. But that didn't exactly matter now. She'd been attacked in her own home and she had no way of knowing if the attacker would try again. Someone had contacted her claiming to have information about payara. Her life had tumbled into this chaos whether she wanted it to or not. The least she could do was take charge of how it all landed.

"I want you to tell me why you said no before," Trent said. "Tell me, point-blank, why you didn't like this cover plan."

She turned to the window and watched the mixture of early morning sun and snow flurries outside. "It doesn't matter anymore."

"It does to me, because this is my case and I'm the one who has to call my boss to explain what's happening and make an official request for your presence on it. Yesterday, I was looking at an entire day to sort that. Now, I've got an hour or less. Not to mention the fact that I've got to prep a partner who made it very clear yesterday that she didn't believe in this assignment and who I have reason to believe doesn't have her head in the game."

She could feel a soft but determined growl building in the back of her throat. "Oh, my head is plenty in the game."

"Then prove it to me," he said. "Convince me that this cover you've now committed us to is the way to go."

"Prove it to you?" she asked. "What is this, high school?"

"No, this is work," he said. Now the growl in her voice was overtaken by the deep rumble in his. "This is the superior officer on a hastily assembled, joint RCMP/ OPP operation, calling rank and asking my colleague to take two minutes to tell me why she objected to my plan, so that everything is aired before we begin."

"Okay, then, *Sir*, if that's the way it's going to be." She spun back, feeling her thick, long mane settle around her shoulders. His eyebrows shot up into his shaggy hairline, as if her use of the word *Sir* had prompted something between alarm and panic. She crossed her arms. "Professionally speaking, I think your plan that I go undercover as Coach Henri's fiancée makes perfect sense. It creates a very easy in-and-out scenario with the minimum amount of suspicion raised. The fact that you already used a photo of me for your cover is a huge bonus. So, professionally speaking, I have no problem at all with the plan. It's a good plan. *Sir.*"

This time, the second "Sir" made his lips turn into a wry smile. "But you shot down the assignment when I first pitched the mission, *Detective*."

"For personal reasons, not professional ones. You're not my supervising officer, we're not in the same branch of law enforcement and I'm on holiday. Turning down a suggested joint mission for personal reasons is completely acceptable."

Was it her imagination or did he just chuckle under his breath? "What were those personal reasons?"

"With all due respect, I don't have to tell you."

"I know you don't, but I'm asking you to, anyway. Chloe, we're friends. Or at least I think we are. I genuinely do care about you." There was something so raw in his voice that she felt something catch in her own throat. "Is there something I'm not getting about pretending to be my fiancée?"

She took a deep breath. "Honestly, I don't like playing the girlfriend role. I never do. You always get to be the strong man. I get to be the arm candy, the doting admirer, the damsel in distress or the pretty little thing under your shoulder."

"Except in this case I'm the mild-mannered hockey coach and you're the daring detective," he said.

A slight smile crossed her lips. Only Trent could manage to be adorable and frustrating at the same time.

"True," she said. "But, still, you command respect just by walking into a room. People always look at you and see a big, handsome guy, oozing with authority. They look at you and see a leader. Nobody thinks you need to be rescued. You do the rescuing.

"All too often, people look at me and underestimate me because I'm a woman. I'm not taken as seriously, and that seems to happen even more when it's my job to play a girlfriend role. It pushes my buttons.

"Growing up, my father used my sister and me like props to bolster his image. I hated it. Do I see the potential, as a detective, in pretending to be Coach Henri's fiancée? Absolutely. But that doesn't mean I'm always going to like it." She took another deep breath and let it out again. "Sir."

"If you call me 'sir' one more time, I'm going back to calling you Lady Cop." Trent ran his hand through his shaggy hair. "You're some piece of work, you know that? I can't imagine anyone thinking you're a damsel, a sidekick or a prop. You know what people are going to think when we walk in a room together? They're going to be amazed a bozo like me could ever be with a woman like you."

She felt herself blush and turned her face back to the window hoping that would hide it. It was his charm coming out, nothing more. Trent was a charming guy. He'd probably inadvertently left a trail of broken hearts all over past undercover missions.

"I promise you, the fact that you're posing as my fiancée won't have any impact on the fact that I see you as an equal partner," he said. "I won't start acting like you're my property. I won't sideline you, take over your conversations or fight your fights for you, unless you ask me to. I won't even try to rescue you unless you're in actual danger. I promise."

That helped. She let out a long breath. "Thank you."

"Now, are you sure that's all it is?" he asked. "Is there anything else you're not telling me?"

What could she possibly say? That he was a good-looking guy and she was really attracted to him? She knew that he wasn't relationship material and that he didn't actually have feelings for her. She did a pretty good job of tamping down her feelings for him and not letting them show. But asking her to spend an entire day, hanging on his arm, pretending to be in love with him?

That might be more than her foolish heart could take.

SIX

"You're the one who taught me every good cover is based on some truth," Chloe said. "Have you ever had a cover that hit a little too close to home?"

He watched as she turned back toward him, her body framed in the early morning light that spilled from the window behind her. There was an earnestness in her face that made him want to pour his heart out on the floor at her feet.

He wanted to tell her what made him so good at pretending to be a gang member was that he understood the anger and pain that welded a heart so firmly shut that eventually all it ended up knowing how to do was to lash out in anger.

He wanted to admit that while she'd been a responsible kid from a messed-up family, he'd been the kind of selfish and irresponsible bad boy who had punched holes in walls, cut classes and broken the hearts of good girls like her.

He wanted to confess that while he'd played several different types of criminals, the hardest thing he'd ever had to do was to pretend to be a more broken and less kind version of himself.

He wanted to tell her all about his family.

He wanted to tell her about his sister, Faith, and how she'd died at the age of twelve because he'd not been there for her when she'd needed him and a killer had grabbed her on her walk home from school.

It was like he couldn't open one door to his past without inevitably opening them all. But if he did, how would she ever look at him the same way again?

"Yeah," he said. "Some covers are definitely harder than others. A three-month stint as a hockey coach is pretty easy. But there've been some that have lasted so long and sunk so deep that I found myself questioning who I really was."

"Well, I can't imagine you've ever started a fight or committed a crime in real life." A mild smile crossed her lips. Then it faded just as quickly. "How do you do it? How do you pretend you're somebody you're not or pretend you don't feel things you do, without it driving you crazy?"

"You're overthinking this," he said. Or maybe he was. "It's just a day. Shut your feelings behind a big metal door and don't let them out until your cover is done." No matter how much he might hear them trying to rattle the doorknob.

He left her alone in her house to get changed and make the phone calls she needed to her superiors, and headed out to his truck. Along with his superiors and hers, he also needed to call the crime scene investigation team to come in and sweep her house. Not that he expected they'd get anything usable. When his calls were done, he stared at his cell phone a long moment, debating dialing one final number.

Lord, I need guidance. There's nobody in the world I trust quite like Jacob.

He dialed. The phone was answered before it had even rung once. "Jacob Henry, RCMP Criminal Investigations."

"Hey, bro." Trent leaned back against the driver's seat and stared up at the ceiling, listening to the sound of heavy snow buffeting the truck. The eldest of the Henry siblings, Jacob was sixteen months older than Trent and half an inch shorter. Jacob had a lot of heart for a cop and a passion for justice. If things had been a lot different when they were younger, they'd probably have been best friends now instead of feeling more like slightly strained, friendly acquaintances. But still, there was nobody Trent respected more. "I'm sorry to bug you about work, but I have a favor to ask."

"Anything." Now that sounded exactly like something Jacob would say.

"As you know, I've been undercover as a hockey coach in Bobcaygeon trying to track down the person who's been making and selling payara. OPP Detective Chloe Brant is helping me on the case now and she was attacked this morning. She's all right and we've already got a team coming to go over the house. There's also a cell phone she recovered from a Gulo that's being processed. I don't know exactly what I'm asking of you. But RCMP Criminal Investigations is a small world..."

"I can keep an eye out," Jacob said. "I can double-check everyone involved in processing physical evidence is on the up and up."

"Thanks." Trent blew out a long breath. Footsteps crunched in the snow outside the truck. He looked up. Chloe was coming down the long drive toward him. She'd changed into a tailored wool jacket, blue jeans and smart leather boots. Through the open top buttons, he caught a glimpse of a crisp white dress shirt and navy blazer. Her hair was tied back in a long, loose braid with wisps falling down around her face. She looked absolutely perfect.

"Chloe Brant is the red-haired detective, right?" Jacob said. "This'll be your third joint operation."

"Fourth, actually," Trent said. He couldn't remember what he'd told Jacob about Chloe. But he could hear that same admiration in Jacob's voice that most people had when they mentioned her. He wasn't sure if that was because of some outside knowledge or something he'd said.

"Have you told her about your new undercover mission?" Jacob said. "The one Mom and Dad might not be too happy about?"

Yeah, nothing like ruining family Christmas like showing up and announcing that he was going to disappear again the first week of January. And this time he would be totally disappearing.

North Jewels Diamond Mine was located in a very remote area of Canada's arctic. Rumors had been rumbling for years that someone had secretly been siphoning diamonds from its operations to fuel organized crime. Proving it and taking them down could cripple multiple crime rings, including the Wolfspiders. It would mean weeks of specialized mining training and cutting off all external contacts for months, maybe even a year or more. A mining operation was a tight ship, ironically to prevent the kind of smuggling he'd be there to investigate. All his communication could be spied on. His belongings could be searched. He would need to go dark.

This time he wouldn't even have a picture of Chloe on his phone to gaze at.

Chloe opened the passenger's-side door and hopped in.

"I've got to go. Talk soon." He ended the call, slid his phone into his pocket and turned to Chloe. The thought of telling her about Jacob flitted across his mind. But Chloe was all detective. Admitting he had one brother would just lead to questions about his two younger brothers, his parents and the sister he'd once had. That was more than a can of worms. That was opening up an entire worm farm. "Good to go?"

"Absolutely." If Chloe had any lingering hesitation about the investigation, her eyes didn't betray it. She reached out her slender, gloved hand. He took it in his and shook it. His hand lingered on hers and he could feel the smooth curve of her pretend engagement ring under the leather. Then he dropped her hand, put the truck into Drive and pulled out onto the snowy rural highway. Chloe pulled out her cell and opened it to a note-taking application. "Okay, tell me the plan."

"My first class is at nine thirty this morning," he said. He could feel himself grinning but wasn't exactly sure why. "Basically it's a physical education and sports psychology class. I get a quick lunch and then go to my second lecture. Then we go grab a very early dinner with the entire team at Nanny's Diner.

"The owner, Eli Driver, also owns the coffee stand at the sports center and works part-time for the college as the hockey team's assistant coach. He's not the easiest man to deal with and doesn't have a lot of time for weaker players. Although we do have Eli to thank for the fact that we can isolate the person who left the payara bag in the locker room to being one of the third-line players. He was running practice a few months back, got frustrated, and decided to make the four of them stay behind after practice and skate laps. He just left them there. Janitors didn't even realize they were still in there until they turned off the lights and heard the guys hollering to turn them back on. They'd already locked up the locker room and had to reopen it."

"And sometime between reopening the locker room for the third-line players and locking it back up again after them, a baggie of drugs appeared?" Chloe asked.

"Pretty much," Trent said. "Like I told you, I've spent three months trying to get chummy with Third Line and so far have discovered diddly-squat. Third Line at Trillium is more like a designation for trouble players and, because there's only four of them, it's not even a full line.

"Aidan's the center. He's a good guy and a natural leader. The rest of the guys would follow him anywhere. He's at Trillium on a full scholarship and when his grades started slipping he couldn't keep up Eli's demands to stay in the first line. He lives with his mother and I get the impression that money's a big problem for them."

"A big enough problem that he'd sell payara to keep a roof over his mom's head?" Chloe asked. She was typing notes on her phone. He was amazed her thumbs could move that fast.

"Maybe," he admitted. "But he's a genuinely good guy, so he'd have to be pretty desperate."

"Any female friend or girlfriend who could be Trilly?"

"Not that I know of. Not that I claim to know everything about the players' social lives. Brandon is the only Third Line player with a sister."

"You mean Lucy." Chloe's smile tightened. "You think she's Trilly and the man she's protecting is her brother, Brandon, or Frank himself? Because she didn't sound like she was talking about a grandfather."

"No, she didn't," he admitted. Not that it wouldn't tie things in a neat and tidy package if Trilly had been calling about the uncomfortably anxious staff sergeant. "To be honest, Brandon is a good guy, too. He tries very hard. I can't imagine him selling drugs. How did Frank seem when you talked to him yesterday?"

"Uncomfortable and distracted." Chloe frowned. "I don't get it. He was always so stern and focused when I worked with him. Not warm, but professional." Her jaw set. "Then again, he's still mourning the loss of his wife. That has to be hard on anyone."

There was something impressive about her trust and loyalty, even if he thought it was misplaced.

"Now, Hodge is dating Poppy, and she was there yesterday," she added. "She could be Trilly. What can you tell me about him?"

"Hodge is your typical potentially strong guy who just needs to brush up his skills. He was suspended already for fighting—"

"He seemed shy," Chloe interjected.

"He is. He's a sweet kid, actually, with impulse-control problems. He gets frustrated too easily, especially when people taunt him. Contact sports are great for a person like that because it gives them a healthy outlet. If a gang had ever gotten their claws into him, he'd have made a great enforcer. Get him worked up enough and point him at someone, and he'll charge like a bull. But I can't imagine him masterminding a drug-dealing operation."

He looked straight ahead through the windshield. Royd of the Wolfspiders was an enforcer, too.

"I could see Poppy being Trilly," Chloe said. "Hodge would be the logical person for her to want to protect. I didn't get the impression she liked that blowhard from the Haliburton team, Johnny, enough to want to protect him. It was more like he was relentlessly trying to impress her. He tried to flirt with both of us."

"If Johnny's involved, it wouldn't explain why the payara only appeared after Third Line was in the locker room," Trent said. "He's a braggart who hits on a lot of women and thinks a lot of himself. I can definitely imagine him dealing drugs. But we'd still need some connection to Trillium College and Third Line."

He eased the truck to a stop at an intersection.

"Can't tell you much about Milo," he added, "except

that he's studying electrical engineering and is really into fixing and building things. He's very quiet and keeps to himself."

"Do, you think Nicole could be Trilly?" she asked.

"Honestly, I think the idea of a fellow cop calling you to report that she knows of a secret drug cover-up is too good to be true," he admitted. Snow crunched beneath the tires. "But it's very possible. Maybe another cop is working with the drug dealers, or being bribed to look the other way, or is somehow compromised by the payara investigation. She could be afraid of the damage it will do to her career if she reports a superior officer. I know you're afraid that if Butler is found to be corrupt they're going to reopen and reexamine all the old cases you worked on together. But, trust me, you can't underestimate the amount of damage a single bad apple can do."

"In my experience, actual bad apples are so rare they're almost a myth," Chloe said. "Cops are human. People make mistakes. But have you ever actually met a rotten-to-the-core cop who used their position to break the law?"

His mouth twisted into a grimace. Knew one? One of his cover identities had meant pretending to be one. "You don't think Frank Butler would bungle an investigation to protect Brandon?"

Chloe stared out through the windshield. "The Frank Butler I served under was a stone-cold sergeant who'd send his own grandson to jail."

* * *

Trent lapsed into silence again. Whatever she'd said to trigger him this time, their conversation was over again for now. She glanced at him sideways.

When she'd first met Trent, it had been in the middle of summer. He'd been undercover with the Wolfspiders and had met her in a dingy roadside diner to pass off information he'd gathered from Uncle. His black hair had been buzzed short that day and soaked with sweat. The strong lines of his form had been perfectly framed by a plain white T-shirt that cut across his broad chest and muscular shoulders, like something carved out of marble.

Trent had looked like danger then. It had radiated from him in every move and every glance. He'd looked like the kind of man she'd have to be on her defenses against. The kind who'd pull a gun on her the moment her guard was down. The kind she'd inevitably find herself tossing to the ground and handcuffing before carting him off the jail. His current beard and toque softened him. It made him look like the kind of caring man who'd hold a steady job, make sure the bills got paid, remember to empty the dishwasher and play with the kids after school. It made Trent look like the kind of man she'd never thought she'd ever have in her life, let alone a future with.

A sign welcoming them to Bobcaygeon appeared ahead. Trent navigated the main streets, until he reached Trillium Community College. The building was smaller than she remembered. It was brown and flat, spread out in three rectangles, with a parking lot to the side and a forest to the back. How had she felt about starting courses here? Determined. Like Trillium was just one more challenge she'd needed to get through to be where she wanted to be.

Trent's hand brushed her shoulder. "Ready?"

"Absolutely." She met his eyes. So what if shivers were moving through her arms again? She could handle shivers. "We've got this."

The afternoon passed in an unending series of seemingly unremarkable encounters. She'd showed her fake engagement ring off to the staff in the office and hung on Trent's arm when they'd paused to grab coffee in the staff room. She'd sat in the very back of the room at his first lecture and listened as Trent talked about how the body reacted to adrenaline and danger. His facts were bang on and all stuff they'd learn at the academy. But his delivery was dry, stilted even. She'd never known Trent to be anything close to stilted.

She'd spotted Poppy in the second row, in a clump of Trillium players that included Hodge, Aidan and the shortest of the third-line players, who she knew by the process of elimination had to be Milo. But besides a sunny smile from Poppy and quick hello from the players, none of them had wanted to stick around to chat.

First class was followed by a quick trip through the cafeteria, where she spotted Lucy in the corner, curled up by herself with a textbook on perfume and cosmetics. Chloe waved. Lucy smiled shyly and waved back. Yes, Chloe remembered hiding in the corner to study all too well.

Milo was also in Trent's next lecture, as were a clump of first- and second-line players, although she noticed that Milo didn't sit anywhere near them. Once again, while technically accurate, Trent's delivery was so awkward it was like he was a robot who'd never spoken to people before. He wasn't connecting. Most of the class wasn't even listening. It was beyond baffling. How could a man of such endless talents and irresistible personality be so terrible at talking to students?

Class finished. Students fled the room and new students filed in, like two currents moving at once. Trent tossed his arm lightly around her shoulder. His face bent toward her. "See anything interesting?"

"Plenty." She smiled benignly as he planted a light kiss on her cheek. "Nothing suspicious."

"Well, let's get out of here." His voice rose to a normal level. "I've just got to grab my stuff and then let's head to Nanny's Diner. I don't know about you, but I'm starving."

They navigated the hallways and he steered her into an office barely larger than a walk-in closet, with a large glass door looking out into the hallway on one side and a huge glass window looking out into the trees on the other. There, on his desk, sat their picture. They were standing on a ski gondola, with snowy, tree-lined slopes spread out beneath them. His arms were around her waist. She was leaning back into the strength of his chest. The smiles on their lips and twinkles in their eyes were so convincing they looked to anyone like a real couple in love. It was all so fake. Yet looked so real. Right down to the piece of costume jewelry on her finger.

"How are you holding up?" Trent's voice was soft behind her. Then she felt the warmth of his hands on her shoulders as his strong fingers squeezed the knots and tension from her muscles.

"I'm good." She stepped forward, out of his hands, and turned around. The office was so small she was practically sitting against the desk with her knees inches from his legs. "Nothing major that stands out. But, to be honest, today was all about maintaining our cover before I meet up with Trilly tonight. I'm really pinning all my hopes on what happens at the hockey game." Maybe Trent would be more engaged with the players then and less like the stiff and awkward oddity she'd seen in front of the class.

"You're frowning," Trent said. "You had that same pained look on your face when I was teaching. Care explaining why?"

He was looking at her intently and she was torn between the desire to be honest and the desire to be polite. She knew which one Trent would prefer. "Your choice on how to play Coach Henri was really odd to me. It wasn't anything like any other cover I'd ever seen you do before."

"Well, of course. Because Coach Travis Henri is a college professor and hockey coach. He doesn't have a shaved head and a motorcycle, with an illegal-looking shotgun on the back."

"He's boring and stiff," she said. His eyes widened. "And that has nothing to do with the fact that he's a professor. I know you, Trent. I've seen how many incarnations of you so far? Four? Five? And you know what each of them had in common? They were likable. They were dynamic. But, Coach Henri—"

"Is boring." He finished the sentence for her.

"Well, maybe I wouldn't want to put it that bluntly—"

"You just did."

She ran both hands through her hair and felt her elbows graze his folded arms. "You said yourself that you had trouble connecting with people on this assignment and getting the players to trust you."

His brow furrowed. His mouth opened.

The window behind her exploded.

SEVEN

Glass showered the room around them. Trent pulled her into his arms and spun her around. They hit the floor. She landed on her elbows and knees. Trent crouched over her, one arm around her waist and the other on her shoulder, cradling her and sheltering her with his body. Freezing wind whipped at them through the broken window. She glanced back, past Trent's forearm. The window had completely shattered.

"You okay?" he asked softly. His fingers touched the back of her neck. It was comforting and protective.

"Yeah, I'm fine," she said. Except for the fact that her heart was racing. He'd grabbed her, reached for her, sheltered her and pulled her from danger. She flexed her legs to stand.

"Hang on. Don't move." Trent's deep voice filled her ear. He braced himself with one hand, slid his other hand into his pocket and pulled out a leather glove. He tugged it on with his teeth and then picked something up off the floor. He held it so she could see it. "See this?"

She looked down. A smooth, symmetrical white stone

lay in his palm, wet from the snow. Smudged words were scrawled on the surface in black marker that was quickly running into an illegible smear.

Mind your own business or your fiancé dies!

Someone was threatening to kill Trent? She nodded. He slid the rock into his pocket. Then he stood, and she let him pull her to her feet.

Jagged edges of glass stood around the window frame. The tree-lined lot was empty. Whoever had pitched the rock through the window had bolted. On the other side of them, a handful of students now stood around the office doorway, although Chloe was amused to see that even more were moving past blithely. Most of the students who had noticed the broken glass were now taking pictures with their phones.

"Now, everyone step back!" Trent said. "Don't want anybody cutting themselves. Can somebody run and let the office know what happened? They're going to want to call the police and send down Maintenance." Students stepped back. A few were typing on their phones, but none were specifically dialing. Then she noticed the young man, with a thin frame and serious eyes, slip away at the back of the crowd. She glanced at Trent. He'd noticed him, too.

"Hey, Brandon!"

The young man froze and, for a moment, she thought he was about to bolt. Instead he took a step toward them. "Hey, Coach! What happened to the window?"

"Somebody threw a rock through it!" Trent said.

"Just glad nobody was hurt. Can you do me a huge favor and call your grandfather?"

Brandon hesitated. His eyes darted from the floor to the broken window and then back to the floor again. "You don't have to call him, though, right? You can just call the division and they'll send a regular cop."

Was it her imagination or was sweat actually forming on the young man's brow?

"Well, somebody should call the police, right?" Trent's arm slid around Chloe's shoulder. "Your grandfather worked with Chloe years ago, so I figured he might want to handle it personally."

Trent pulled her in for a hug. But she could tell in an instant that he was doing so to position himself so that they could whisper without being heard. Yes, this kind of Trent hug she knew well and had experienced before. It was all tactics and no warmth, unlike the confusing way his fingers had touched her skin after the home invasion. Trent rested his head on top of hers. She tucked her head into his neck.

"They used an erasable whiteboard marker on a wet rock," he said softly. "The rock is from one of the planters out front. The marker could be from any classroom. It's a total crime of opportunity." She could hear the frown in his voice. "Thankfully, it gives us an opportunity for you to talk to Butler about the payara situation, and judge where he's at with that for yourself. Certainly, I think something's off with him. But you might disagree. When he gets here, I'll talk to him and then I'll make myself scarce while you talk to him. We can compare notes afterward."

"Sounds good." A sigh of relief filled her body and she found herself moving deeper into Trent's chest before she caught herself and pulled back.

Trent detangled himself and walked over to talk to Brandon. By the sound of things, Brandon still hadn't called the police but was reluctantly agreeing to give Trent his grandfather's cell phone number.

Chloe turned back to the glass-strewed office. A silent prayer of thanks crossed her lips. She was more than grateful Trent had suggested she talk to Butler alone. She was almost surprised at the thoughtfulness of it. A larger task force would inevitably be formed to investigate the payara situation in the future, even if Butler didn't face an internal affairs investigation.

Trent's undercover mission into the third-line players was just the first step of a much broader and larger operation that would be launched. Her conversation with the staff sergeant after the Gulos' attack on the sports center had been rushed. Her top priority had been protecting Trent's cover, even though she barely understood it, so her own reasons for being there had fallen completely by the wayside. But now, thanks to a rock through the window and its hastily scrawled message, she had the opportunity to have a real conversation with her former training officer about the whole situation without threatening Trent's investigation.

"Clo?" Trent's hand brushed her shoulder. She turned. He was holding out his cell phone. His brow furrowed and she could tell by the set of his jaw that he was working at finding the right words to say. "I'm going to head to the front office and fill them in on what's going on. Brandon's grandfather says filing a report over the phone is fine for vandalism. But I wondered if you wanted to talk to him, too? You know, cop to cop."

Really? Trent handed her the phone. She took it. "Hello, Staff Sergeant Butler?"

"Detective Brant." The older officer's voice was rushed and breathless, like he'd been interrupted while running on a treadmill. "I understand you want to talk to me about the vandalism at Trillium College?"

She stepped deeper into Trent's office. Glass crunched under her feet. Cold air stung her skin.

"It goes much deeper than that, Sir," she said. "Are you free at all this afternoon? I'd really appreciate being able to talk to you about it in person."

"It's my day off, Detective. My grandson should never have given his coach my personal number. A vandalism report can be filed directly with the division. I hope you have a nice day—"

"But, Sir, it was a threat. There was a warning written on the rock. The words were pretty smudged but I was able to make them out."

"What did it say?" he asked. Was it her imagination or had his tone grown sharper?

"'Mind your own business or your fiancé dies,'" she said.

"Mind your own business about what?"

She didn't know. But it wasn't a big stretch to presume it had something to do with the payara and maybe even her secretive informant, Trilly.

"I don't know for sure, but I suspect the fact that I

cleared out the Gulos from the sports center yesterday has something to do with it. It was clear they were looking for payara." She waited for him to answer. Instead a long pause waited on the phone line. "Look, Sir. It's no secret that a baggie of payara was found in the sports center a few months ago. Rumors are swirling around other divisions that the investigation is stalled, and it's been leaked to the press. You and I have worked together well in the past, I know this area well and I'm already on the ground. I'd like to be considered for a transfer to work on this case or at least to be more involved in the investigation of what happened yesterday."

Another pause filled the line. Suddenly a memory came back to her mind of standing awkwardly in a small meeting room as Butler reprimanded her sternly and at length for some minor mistake she'd made. He hadn't ever been a warm man when they'd worked together. He'd been downright cold at times. But he'd been incredibly professional, his standards had been high, and at that time in her life she'd appreciated that.

"Thank you for your offer, Detective," Butler said, "but I assure you all of our active cases are well staffed within the division, and I'm not in the habit of commenting on ongoing investigations. Have a good afternoon."

The call ended. She turned back. Trent was gone, but Brandon still stood there, one arm crossed in front of his chest. "Coach said he'd meet you in the head office. I'll show you the way."

"Thank you," she said.

He walked with her to the office, in silence, his lanky form dipping with each step like he was self-consciously trying to shrink. She tried to do some quick mental math to figure out how old he must've been when she'd worked with his grandfather. Six maybe? Seven? Yet none of her memories of Butler had included pictures of his grandchildren on his desk, or a small family visiting the office. "I worked with your grandfather a long time ago. He was a good man to train under. He was very hard on rookies."

Brandon nodded. "He has pretty high standards, yeah."

The question was, had her standards been too low? Had she been so eager for her life to have some order and structure that all it had taken to win her admiration was a cold demeanor and strict dedication to the rules?

She found Trent in the head office talking to a slender, blond, uniformed cop.

"Constable Docker, right?"

"Call me Nicole." She turned. "Nice to see you again."

"That was fast." Chloe reached out to shake her hand before realizing it was holding an evidence bag containing the white, smudged rock.

"Oh, I was just around the corner when the call came in." Guilt flickered in Nicole's eyes, so quickly it was almost unnoticeable. Guilt about what? What was around the corner from Trillium exactly besides the sports center?

Chloe smiled and nodded, then stood back to let Nicole take their statements.

It was her first real, hard look at her beyond a very quick introduction they'd had at the sports center yesterday, when Chloe had been looking for Butler. She'd have pegged Nicole to be in her early twenties. The rookie cop had curly blond hair scraped back into a ponytail at the nape of her neck and the kind of bright blue eyes Chloe had longed for as a preteen.

"If you're free, I'd love to grab a coffee and talk more," Chloe said. "Staff Sergeant Butler was my training officer when I was a rookie, too. I'm sure we have a lot in common."

Was it her imagination or did slight panic flicker in Nicole's eyes?

"I'm sure you would both enjoy that." Trent's arm slid over Chloe's shoulder. "But sadly, my fiancée and I have to hurry over to Nanny's Diner. The whole team is waiting for us. Maybe you two gals can meet up at the game." He practically steered Chloe out of the office and toward the front door.

The winter sun sunk low in a pale gray sky. Their footsteps crunched across the snow-covered parking lot. His head bent toward hers. "I appreciate your impulse to chase leads, Detective. But for today you're my fiancée, and we are on a very tight timeline. Not showing up at Nanny's for the team meal would raise some pretty major eyebrows." They reached his truck. He slid his arm off her shoulder and opened her door for her. "If it's any help, I did find out she's single."

Chloe felt her eyebrows rise. "How did you find that out?"

Trent chuckled and walked around to his side of the truck. He whistled something musical under his breath. If he was trying to make her jealous by implying Nicole had asked him out, it wasn't going to work. But that would explain why she'd looked vaguely guilty. He hopped into the driver's side and looked at her. She had no idea what the expression on her face was, but whatever it was made him laugh.

"Don't worry. I'd never date a cop who tried to arrest me without first reading me my rights." He draped his hand over the back of her seat and backed up. "Even if she had, I don't have time for a girlfriend. I simply don't date or do relationships."

An odd heaviness settled into the pit of her stomach. She wasn't sure why. Trent had never showed any interest in dating her, with the one notable exception of the coffee date that wasn't. Surely the knowledge he didn't date anybody at all would make her feel better.

"I spoke to Staff Sergeant Butler," she said. "It was disappointing. I asked him if I could assist on the payara case, and he was curt. But I still don't like thinking he's a bad cop. His standards were insanely high. I can't imagine he'd be open to blackmail or greed, or allow corruption in his ranks."

"You can't make blanket statements about bad cops. Like you said, cops are human and make mistakes." Trent pulled onto the road and drove. His hand remained on the back of her seat. His fingertips brushed the back of her neck. "But I wouldn't blame you for being miffed that he wouldn't come down to the college. Your life was threatened, after all."

"Miffed?" She pushed his hand off her seat back, feeling the tension his hand had begun to brush away snap back with a vengeance. "Trent, I'm a cop. I've had my life threatened more times than I can count, in far more disturbing and graphic ways. Besides, it was your life that was threatened. Not mine. Even with the marker smudges, it was pretty clear they wrote 'fiancé' with one *e*, not two."

"Because criminals are such great spellers," he said. "They threw the rock in my office window—"

"When we were both in clear view of the window. I haven't left your side all day, so it's not like it would be easy to threaten me alone. I'm the cop. You're the mild-mannered hockey coach."

"You left out 'boring,'" he added.

"I'm sorry if using that word bothered you," she said. "But you were incredibly awkward and uncomfortable just being in that lecture hall."

He didn't answer. Instead he just stared straight ahead, with both hands on the steering wheel, as they drove through the small-town streets.

It had been an act, right? She'd seen him face down armed criminals without so much as breaking a sweat. So it was hard to imagine being in front of a classroom would intimidate him.

He pulled into the parking lot of Nanny's Diner. They got out of the truck and walked toward the blue-and-white-striped awnings.

Two people stood near the entrance, arguing by the look of things, and it took Chloe's eyes a moment to realize what she was really seeing.

Lucy stood in the doorway, dressed in a waitress's apron and holding two jugs of pop as if someone had called her to the door while she was waiting tables. A tall man with gray hair and a baseball cap was talking to her, his hands shaking in the air and his voice a low hiss. It was clear whatever he was saying was upsetting her almost to the point of tears.

What was this? Chloe's footsteps quickened, feeling Trent match pace.

"As long as I'm paying for your schooling, young lady, you're staying in Bobcaygeon and going to Trillium, and that's final!" The elderly man's voice rose.

Chloe's heartbeat stuttered. It was Frank Butler. The staff sergeant didn't seem to notice their approach. "I don't care how many letters you get that university in Vancouver to send about deferring your acceptance. You are not going. Makeup making or perfume mixing, or whatever it is you call it, is a garbage waste of an education and I'm not throwing my good money away on it! Period."

"Good afternoon, Frank," Trent said loudly. Their footsteps paused in the snow. Then his voice dropped softly. "Hi, Lucy."

Lucy looked up nervously and the tears in the young woman's eyes shook something inside Chloe's chest. Had her former training officer always been so volatile?

Frank turned and stumbled as his foot slipped in the snow.

"Afternoon," he said and nodded curtly without meeting their eyes. The unmistakable stench of liquor rose from his breath. He walked off.

Lucy paused for a moment, turned and bolted into the diner. The door swung shut behind her.

Chloe turned to Trent. "I had no idea Butler drank. Did you?"

* * *

"No, I didn't." Trent's head shook. "But, the only time I saw him out of uniform was at hockey games and I kept enough of a distance not to notice the smell of whatever was in his thermos."

He sighed. If Butler had a drinking problem, it would certainly go a long way in explaining how he'd botched a crucial investigation and why he was so jittery. Despite what Chloe might've hoped, an internal investigation would be for the best, especially if it got the staff sergeant the help he needed.

Trent turned to Chloe and reached for her hand, ready to walk with her into the diner. To his surprise, as his fingers brushed hers, he could feel her shaking beneath his touch. He pulled her close.

"Are you okay?" he asked quietly.

"I just can't believe I never saw it," Chloe said. "My father was the same. He was one way in public and another in private. I could never understand how he fooled people. But he was very charming and outgoing, and Butler was this cold, hard stickler for rules…" Her voice trailed off.

"Listen to me," he said, "everybody has ugly and unpleasant parts of themselves that they try not to show to the wider world. It's possible Butler might not have been like that when you worked with him. Sometimes grief hits people hard. Or early onset dementia can cause angry outbursts and emotional issues. You can't know. We shouldn't guess without knowing more. And you definitely can't blame yourself for not knowing."

Even though he could tell that, in a way, she was.

Lord, I don't know what she's lived through or what battles she's fighting on the inside. Please, heal her heart. Please, help me help her.

She met his eyes and smiled weakly. There was a slight quiver to her lips that made something thud inside his chest.

"Maybe," she said. "I'm just suddenly doubting everything I thought I knew about him. Sometimes when you've seen the very worst side of someone it changes everything and there's no going back from that."

Yeah, that's what he was afraid of.

They pushed through the door to the diner. His hand was still loosely holding hers and he told himself it was all for the sake of his cover and not because of how comfortably her palm fit into his.

He scanned the room. Most of the Trillium hockey players were crammed into three large, yellow-vinyl booths in their usual place at the far side of the wall.

Aidan looked up and waved. There was an unmistakable tension in the third-line center's face, and he wasn't the only member of the team who was scowling. What was that all about? Trent waved back. Then he leaned toward Chloe and whispered, "Game time."

They started across the floor through the tables. But they'd barely taken five steps when a burst of arrogant laughter to his right made his head turn. He frowned.

A couple of the Haliburton players were lounging at a tall table by the jukebox, cracking jokes under their breath and tossing glances in his players' direction.

The Haliburton coach was a foulmouthed man who'd never really done much to encourage sportsmanlike behavior from his players, as far as Trent could see. It wasn't the first time a couple of players from their rival team had wandered into Nanny's before a game looking to psych his players out and goad them into a fight, or even just to test how long they could hang out and talk nonsense before Eli got frustrated and kicked them out.

It was an immature posturing thing that had been going on for far longer than Trent had been on the scene, and he got the impression that with the number of regional hockey teams that bussed in to practice at the Bobcaygeon rink and college students from neighboring towns that drove over to work out at the elite sports center, Eli couldn't exactly afford to refuse to serve them all. Trent was just thankful his guys were usually too good to take the bait.

"That's Johnny." Chloe gestured subtly to the blond jock. "He's the guy who was in the exercise room yesterday with Poppy."

He nodded. "I figured. The other player's the Haliburton goalie. His name is George."

The ice cubes rattled in Lucy's jug as she poured pop into their glasses. George ran his eyes over her and snickered. It was an ugly sound. Then Johnny leaned over and whispered something in Lucy's ear. Her cheeks went crimson.

"Hey, Johnny!" The tone in Chloe's voice told Trent she'd noticed the interaction, too. "I see you made it out safe and sound yesterday."

"Detective!" He stood and glanced at her hand holding Trent's. "You didn't tell me you had a boyfriend."

There was a hint of reproach in his voice. Trent didn't

much like the sound of it. But at least now Lucy had stepped away from them and moved on to another table.

Trent leaned his head toward Chloe, keeping his mouth close enough to her ear that they were unlikely to be overheard. "Do you want me to handle this?"

Chloe snorted and shook her head. "No. Thanks. Let me. After all, he might have seen something, yesterday." She pulled her hand out of his and stepped toward the Haliburton players.

"Coach Henri is my fiancé, actually," Chloe said. "I hope all that chaos at the sports center didn't throw you off your game. I'm looking forward to seeing our team beat yours fair and square."

A smattering of laughter came from the Trillium players.

Johnny's eyebrow quirked.

Trent grit his teeth as he felt something fierce and protective rise up inside him. He didn't like the way this student, fifteen years his junior, was looking at Chloe.

God, I know I should ignore him, just like I always tell my players to. I promised Chloe that I wouldn't fight her fights for her. And if I tell a college student off for looking at Chloe the wrong way, I'm going to end up looking like a possessive jerk in her eyes.

"You sure she's a cop?" George pivoted in his seat. "She doesn't look that tough to me."

"Oh, yeah." Johnny sniggered, like he didn't believe it, either. "Apparently she took down a knife-wielding gang member in an elf mask."

"Her?" The goalie looked Chloe up and down. "Nah,

that didn't happen. What she do? Throw her purse at him?"

So, this was what it was like being a female officer. Sure, Trent had heard the stories from women he'd served alongside about dealing with a steady stream of disrespect from stupid punks, but still he'd never gotten over the shock of seeing it firsthand.

George slid off his seat, grabbed a dull butter knife off the table and waved it around theatrically, like a bad television ninja, complete with sound effects. "Watch out, girlie. I'm a mean gang elf and I'm coming to stab you!"

A grin turned on Chloe's lips. She stepped forward, knocked the knife from the young man's grasp with one hand and caught his wrist with the other. Then she spun him around, twisting his arm behind his back and forcing him down until he was kneeling on the floor.

The Haliburton goalie swore and looked up at Trent. "Tell her to let go!"

"You'll have to talk to her. I don't tell her what to do." Trent chuckled. He could hear a smattering of laughter and the murmur of gasps coming from the Trillium players. "Looked to me like you just threatened to stab a cop in front of a room full of witnesses."

"Coach Henri!" Eli rushed through the diner toward them. "What is going on? I was on the phone and suddenly one of the waitresses comes rushing into the office in saying there's a fight about to break out."

Chloe let go of the goalie. He scowled, stood and stuffed his hands into his pockets.

"Not a fight," Trent said. "One of the Haliburton

players was acting foolish and waving a knife around. My fiancée stepped in before the situation could escalate."

Eli nodded to Chloe. "Thank you."

She smiled. "No problem."

Trent stepped back and watched as Eli escorted Johnny and George from the diner. The chorus of Trillium players laughing and clapping behind them seemed to be growing. Then, to his surprise, Chloe threw her arms around him and hugged him tightly. His hands slid about her waist.

"That was fun," she whispered. "Thank you."

"For what?" he asked. "For letting you take down some arrogant college kid? You asked me to let you handle it, so I did."

"I know." She looked up into his eyes. Something sparkled there, like happiness mingled with gratitude. "I also know just how badly you were itching to jump in and take over. It was written all over your face."

Well, he'd made the right decision by the sound of it. The applause had turned into a thunderous wave of students stomping on the floor and banging on the tables. Her hands slid up around his neck. He found himself pulling her closer into his chest. "I think they're chanting for me to kiss you."

"Do you think you should?" she asked.

They were still whispering, her face just inches from his, although he was certain nobody would be able to make out their words over the sound of the racket his players were making. He could feel his heart beating like a drum in his chest, matching the rhythm of the percussion around him.

"Maybe. If that's okay with you."

What are you doing? the voice of logic shouted in his head, struggling to be heard.

They were on an undercover mission. Yes, they were pretending to be a couple. But the desire to kiss her was stronger than that. He wanted to kiss her for real. Like she was really his. And he was really hers. He couldn't let himself get emotionally compromised like that. Not by her. Not now. Not ever.

She bit her lip, just a little. Then she nodded. "Yeah, I think that's okay."

Her fingers brushed the back of his neck and curled through his hair. He pulled her close. His lips met hers and he kissed her.

EIGHT

Kissing Chloe was like coming home to a place where he'd always hoped to belong. He felt her kiss him back, sweetly and gently. The clapping turned into a roar of applause. Hands banged on the table like the beat of dozens of drums. He could even hear some of his players whistling.

Then Chloe pulled away, ending the kiss. She hugged him, tucking her head into that old familiar and practiced spot on his neck that meant she wanted to talk without being overheard and suddenly the full weight of what he'd done hit him. For the first time, in his entire life, he'd kissed someone not because he'd felt obligated to, or because it was what his cover identity would do, but because he'd wanted to. He tilted his head toward her, thankful for the wall of noise because it would hide his words. "I hope that was okay."

Her breath tickled his ear. "It was the right thing for Coach Henri to do."

But was it the right thing for Detective Trent Henry to do?

She pulled out of his arms, brushed a quick kiss on the scruff of his cheek and sat down in the booth. She flushed, smiling, and waved her hands at the players. "Oh, you guys are being ridiculous! It's like you've never seen a man kiss his fiancée before."

Laughter rippled through the room. Trent sat down. Milo reached across the table and shook her hand. Aidan flashed Chloe a thumbs-up. "I can't believe you took George down like that!"

She laughed. "It was nothing. People like him and Johnny are all bark and no bite."

Eli came over and thanked her. Lucy brought a platter of wings to the table. Then it was like something broke in the air and the players all started talking at once. Watching Chloe take down the rival goalie in the middle of the diner had somehow chipped a hole in the invisible barrier that had always stood between him and the four of them.

Milo told a ridiculous story about trying to talk his way out of a driving ticket when he was fifteen and had borrowed his older brother's car without permission even though he didn't have a license.

Aidan started teasing Hodge about dating Poppy.

Brandon stopped checking his phone.

Conversation flew around the booth as smoothly and easily as a well-passed puck and, for the first time since taking on his cover, he felt like he was really getting to know who these young men were.

When the wings were done and the players started filing out, Trent helped Chloe into her coat and they walked outside. His arm slid around her shoulder again, effortlessly and almost unconsciously, as they walked to his truck. He opened the door for her again, they got in and he peeled out of the parking lot, thankful for the few minutes they'd get alone before they reached the sports center.

"I feel like I should thank you," he said. "I don't know how you did it. Those young men opened up more to you tonight than they ever have to me."

"They felt like I had their back and that I was one of them." She leaned against the seat, looking far more exhausted than he'd expected her to feel. "I don't blame them for being suspicious of people, especially outsiders. If you're right, at least one of them committed a major crime having that much payara in his possession, and at least some of the others are covering for him. If Aidan's involved, it could cost him his scholarship. Hodge already has a record. And judging from how we saw Butler yell at Lucy, I can't blame Brandon for wanting to keep his head down. They have no reason to trust me, you or anyone. They need to know that we have their back and that we're on their side. Or, at least, that we're willing to listen and hear their side of the story."

She was right, of course. He'd even go so far as to say that many of the criminals he met had gone through childhood traumas as bad, or even worse, than the murder of his sister, and talking to them about how he'd gotten lured into petty crime by Royd and snared by the Wolfspiders had helped get them to trust him. But what could he say that would possibly connect with these bright and shiny college students?

I've always hated school, so it feels like I'm suffocat-

*ing every time I walk into Trillium. I have three amaz-
ing brothers and two incredible parents, who I think
have all given up on me. I used to have a sister, too,
but she was strangled to death by some creep when I
was thirteen, because I was hanging behind the school
with idiot Wolfspiders when I was supposed to be walking her home...*

Her hand lay in the empty space between them just
resting on the edge of the console. He resisted the temp-
tation to reach for it. The kiss at the diner had been too
real, at least for him. But she'd kissed Coach Henri. She
hadn't kissed the real him. Like she'd said, once she
knew his entire ugly story, there'd be no going back.

He pulled into the sports center parking lot. "I'm
going to suggest we split up," he said. "I'll go be with
the players. You hang out in the stands. See if you can
strike up a conversation with Nicole. I'll keep an eye
on the clock once the third period starts. When you slip
out, I'll give you exactly fifteen minutes to either text
or reappear. Anything longer than that, I'm putting Eli
in charge and coming out. Okay?"

"Got it," Chloe said. "Hopefully, Trilly will come
through for us and in a few quick hours we'll have
enough information to pass it up the chain of command,
they'll form a task force and authorize a raid and then
it will be out of our hands."

"Agreed." And then what? Then he'd assume another
cover identity and plunge into specialized mining operation training for his next investigation, before flying
off to the remote mine in the Arctic, and he'd be stuck
figuring out how to say goodbye to Chloe again. His

phone started to ring. He glanced down at the name on the screen. Jacob.

"Who's Jacob?" Chloe asked.

"The guy I told you about with RCMP Criminal Investigations. I should take it."

"Understood." Chloe brushed her lips over his cheek, in a gesture he was certain was for the benefit of the gaggle of players and students already gathering in the sports center parking lot, and hopped out of the truck. He tried not to watch the swing of her hair brushing her back as she walked away.

Then he answered the phone. "Hey, bro. What's the news?"

"All good," Jacob said. "Everyone on the team who's processing the cell phone and Detective Brant's house is aboveboard and someone I'd professionally vouch for. If there is a corrupt element impacting your case, it won't come from within our part of the police world."

Thank You, God. Trent sighed and leaned back against the seat. "Thanks, I appreciate it."

"No problem," his brother said. "Mom and Dad are wondering when you're arriving at the farm. The rest of us are here already and tomorrow's Christmas Eve."

Not that Trent needed the reminder. "I'll be there for dinner on Christmas Day."

"Then you're going to disappear." Jacob said it like it was a statement of fact.

So much for thinking they were going to save this argument until Christmas. Then again, the eldest Henry brother had always been the family peacemaker.

"I've spent my whole professional life fighting gang

crime," Trent said. "I'm running around out here, cutting the heads off snakes, only to have six more grow back in their place before I can even turn around. If a diamond mine is funneling money into organized crime, and I can take it out, I'll be chopping down the Wolfspiders, the Gulos and countless other gangs at the roots."

"Those were some impressively mixed metaphors." Jacob chuckled. "But, seriously, why does it have to be you?" Sounded like he really was getting the prefight out before he had to explain it to the folks. Maybe it was Jacob's way of helping.

"Because I'm good at what I do, and I have no relationship entanglements." Not to mention he was really good at closing doors and walking away. "The tech crew is already erasing any trace of me online. I have no digital footprint. The mining company can search my picture online all they'll want and they'll never find me. I'm off the grid. I don't exist. I'll be cut off from the world up there, and I'll be watched constantly. They'll invent a fake relationship for me, a parent most likely, and send me carefully crafted messages from that person with cyphers hidden inside incase of emergencies."

"I know. I looked into that, too," Jacob said. Trent could almost hear him nodding. "Sounds like an impressive investigation. I just know what Mom and Dad are going to say and your voice sounded a bit off when we last talked. I want to make sure that you're sure."

"Of course I'm sure. We can talk a lot more at Christmas. But right now I've got to go."

"Got it," his brother said. "If you need anything, feel free to call."

"Thanks." The call ended. He put his game face on and walked into the sports center, feeling an odd and uneasy ache in his chest. He blamed Jacob. Sure, his older brother meant well, but it wasn't exactly helpful to have him planting doubt in his mind. In a few hours the case would be over, he'd be saying goodbye to Chloe again and she'd never know just how many nights he'd probably end up lying awake on his bunk at night, listening to the sound of dozens of burly men snoring, missing her face.

Trent found the team in the locker room, abuzz with fresh energy and enthusiasm. As much as he enjoyed it, he couldn't help thinking Chloe was the reason why.

They stood in a circle, Trent stuck his hand in the middle of the huddle and they all piled their hands on top. Then the team hit the ice with more hustle than they ever had before. But only half of his mind was on the game. The other half kept glancing up to the stands, instinctively seeking out Chloe's face. She was sitting one row behind Nicole, who was in uniform and with a young male officer. Chloe had somehow also acquired a Trillium College team banner. She waved it at him. He waved back.

Then Chloe glanced at her phone. Her brow furrowed. She gestured to the exit, he nodded, and she slipped out of her seat and disappeared behind the stands. Where was she going? She wasn't supposed to meet the informant until the third period and the game had barely started. A shout broke out from the bench. He spun back just in time to see Hodge haul himself

over the boards and pelt across the ice into the middle
of a face-off, like a cue ball shooting across the table.

"Hodge, what are you doing?" Trent bellowed. "Get
back here!"

But his words were swallowed up in a chant of
"Fight! Fight! Fight!" erupting from the stands as Hodge
ploughed into Johnny.

Hodge grabbed Johnny by the jersey and yanked
him sideways as Johnny's fist ploughed into the side
of his head. The ref's whistle blew. Eli and the coach
from the opposing team were already pelting toward the
scrum. Aidan, Brandon and Milo were tumbling over
the boards, too, yelling at Hodge to stop.

Trent grabbed the boards and leaped over after them,
feeling automatic prayers for wisdom cross his heart as
he strode across the ice. *Lord, what's happening? I've
always known Hodge had issues. But to lose it like this
in the middle of a game?*

Johnny was punching back as good as he got, pum-
meling Hodge with a blistering force that was all brute
strength and no skill. A crowd was forming now as parents, refs and coaches tried to pull them apart. Players
on both teams exchanged pushes and insults as the energy seemed to spread.

Trent grabbed Hodge by the collar with one hand
and Johnny with the other and physically yanked them
apart. Then he straightened his arms, giving just enough
torque on the back of their jerseys to make sure they
felt the pinch, and marched them to the penalty boxes.
He'd broken up wilder fights with killers twice their
size. They were just fortunate he didn't knock their

helmeted heads together. He tossed the guys into opposing penalty boxes.

"Sit!" he ordered. Johnny glared at Hodge. Hodge stared at the ground. Trent could hear Eli, still out on the ice, now bellowing at the other team's coach and the ref. Third-line players skated up and leaned over the boards, waving something at Hodge and yelling. Poppy, Lucy and a handful of other students had run around the stands and yelled at them from the other side, leaving him stuck in the middle.

He didn't have the patience for this level of angst and hormones. His eyes rolled to the stands and Chloe's empty seat. Where was his fake fiancée when he needed her? He just had to pray her meeting with Trilly was going better than this. His eyes locked on Hodge. Hodge's pupils were so large his eyes seemed to bulge. "What did you take? What are you on?"

"Nothing!" Hodge spluttered. "Johnny kissed Poppy! Somebody posted it to social media!"

Johnny swore. "You're a lunatic."

Trent was almost tempted to agree. He'd charged into the middle of a hockey face-off and started throwing punches like a caveman because a known player had kissed his girlfriend? But Trent also didn't believe for a moment that Hodge was sober. Aggression, suggestibility and an adrenaline-like rush, Hodge was practically an advertisement for payara.

"I didn't kiss Johnny!" Poppy's voice rose to a wail. She bent over the railing and tried in vain to grab hold of Hodge's shoulder. "You've gotta believe me! We just work out together!"

Aidan launched himself over the boards almost vertically and pushed a cell into Hodge's hands. Hodge thrust it in Poppy's face.

"Then explain this!" he demanded. A picture filled the screen that sure did look like Johnny and Poppy locking lips. "Why did somebody post this?"

Why did anybody take it? Trent shook his head.

"That's not me!" Poppy shouted. "Someone Photoshopped a picture of Johnny kissing somebody else to look like me and then posted it online!"

"Oh, yeah, that's really logical." Hodge tried to stand. Trent pushed him back down. "Why would somebody do that?"

"Because they're a troll, you're rival teams and they're trying to cause chaos," Trent said. It had worked, too. But was that all it was? A fight had broken out on the ice while Chloe just happened to be meeting her informant, because someone had just happened to post a picture of the girlfriend of the worst hothead on his team kissing one of the opposing team's star players?

"Hodge and Johnny, stay here and don't move," he said. "Now, does anybody want to admit to doping Hodge with payara? Or, Hodge, do you want to admit it yourself?"

Hodge glared and shook his head. Nobody else met Trent's eye. Right.

"Who posted the picture?" he asked.

"I don't know." Hodge grunted.

"Somebody anonymous," Aidan said.

Of course. Trent turned to face the other players.

"Brandon, go grab Hodge's water bottle and bring it

to me," he said. Brandon took off across the ice. "The rest of you, get back to your own bench and sit down. Aidan and Milo, I expect you to set an example. Lucy, take Poppy back to her seat. She can sort things out with Hodge after the game."

Brandon sprinted back with the water bottle. At a glance, Trent could see faint sediment swirling at the bottom.

"Brandon, I'm putting you in charge of that bottle. Hold on to it until Chloe can take it from you. Don't let anybody else so much as touch it until it can be tested by police. Hodge, you're going to need to take a drug test. When Eli stops pushing and shoving the opposing coach, tell him I'll be back in a minute."

He could hear voices clamoring behind him. He didn't look back. Instead, Trent sprinted through the risers, through the change rooms and into the hallway. He checked his phone again as his feet pounded down the hall. Nothing from Chloe. *Lord, please may I be worried about nothing.* He pressed his feet faster, prayers pushing through him with every step. He burst through the emergency exit door and out into the alley. But saw nothing, except garbage cans and piles of snow. *Help me, God. Where is she?*

Then he heard the sounds of a struggle and ran around the corner just in time to see Royd, the very same thug that had introduced him to the Wolfspiders so many years ago, hold a knife against Chloe's throat as he dragged her backward toward a van.

If he tried to stop Royd, his former friend would

recognize him and his cover would be blown. But if he didn't, Chloe would die.

The knife pressed against her skin, threatening to end her life if she made one wrong move. A huge arm tightened over her chest, squeezing the oxygen from her lungs. Her eyes looked up to the snow-filled sky as her neck was forced upward by the prick of the blade digging into her skin. Desperate prayers filled her heart.

It was the same man who'd broken into her house and attacked her. She'd barely seen his face over her shoulder as he'd leaped on her from behind and jammed a weapon into her neck. But everything she'd suspected in the glance had been confirmed with terrifying certainty when she'd smelled the rancid odor of his breath and heard the same rough voice threatening that if she didn't hand over the Gulo's cell phone immediately, he'd take her somewhere remote and hurt her until she told him everything he wanted to know.

"Leave her alone!" Trent's voice seemed to rise on the bitter wind.

"Back off! Or I'll slit her throat right in front of you!"

"She's my woman, Royd!" Trent shouted. What was Trent doing? How did he know her kidnapper? She didn't know if he was blowing his cover just to save her life or because he knew he'd be recognized if he tried to help her. "Did Uncle really give you permission to off a Wolfspider's lady?"

"Trent?" Royd swore. His voice shook with disbelief and rage. "Nah, it can't be. I gotta be seeing things."

Confusion bordering on panic threatened to steal

her breath from her lungs. How did this criminal know Trent's name? None of this made any sense. But she could also feel the knife had slipped an inch away from her skin. Barely more than a breath lay between her and the weapon. But it was all the space she needed.

Chloe jammed her thumbs between her throat and the knife handle, prying the blade away from her body just long enough to pivot sideways and wrench the knife from his grasp. They struggled for the knife, even as she could hear Trent's footsteps pelting across the ground toward them. She wrenched the blade from Royd's grasp. His fist made contact with her jaw, filling her eyes with stars and knocking her body to the ground. She fell hard on the frozen cement. Royd loomed over her. She kicked up at him, forcing him back. Trent's footsteps grew closer.

Royd hesitated. Then he turned and ran.

"Chloe!" Trent dropped to the pavement beside her. "Are you hurt?"

"No, I'm okay. Thanks." She gasped. "Trilly texted and said she needed to meet me right away. I ran outside and into a trap. Who is that man? Why does he know your name?"

"He's a Wolfspider I crossed paths with in the past." Worry pooled in the depths of his eyes, making something ache inside her chest.

Something was wrong. Very wrong. The man who'd broken into her home was somebody Trent knew. The informant she'd planned to meet had turned out to be a trap.

Trent was still kneeling beside her in the snow. His

fingers brushed her hair from her face and warmth filled her body. This whole mess had become intensely and dangerously personal. Trent had kissed her. He'd held her. She'd been emotionally compromised. She'd just been reminded yet again how little she knew Trent. And it had put her life in danger and blown his cover.

She shoved his hand away. "What are you doing? Go! Go after him! Don't let him get away!"

Trent blinked and it was like a switch had flicked inside his mind. Then he leaped to his feet and sprinted after Royd. "Stay back unless I give the signal! Stay out of sight if you can. Don't let him see you!"

"Will do." She stumbled to her feet and forced herself after him. Trent would need her for the arrest. He could hardly do so himself without blowing his cover.

Her body ached. Her head swam. She watched as Royd yanked a van door open and leaped in. She heard the sound of the engine turn over. Trent yanked him from the front seat and tossed him to the ground. Royd swung back hard, and then it was a battle of blows and limbs. She slipped around to the other side of the van, staying low and out of sight, hiding from Royd's gaze as Trent forced him to the icy ground.

"What are you doing here?" Trent pinned him there with his forearm over his throat. "What do you know about payara?"

Royd swore and barked out a laugh, like he was staring down something that was anything but funny. "I could ask you the same thing. Are you really involved with that cop?"

As she watched, it was like Trent's body transformed

in front of her. His shoulders drew back wider. His jaw-
line tightened and a colder, meaner look than she'd ever
seen before filled his eyes. Did Trent know she was
there, close and listening in? Surely he had to know she
would be. "Don't make me ask you again. If we didn't
have history together, I wouldn't be asking so nicely."

Royd's eyes narrowed. "I'm not talking till you tell
me why you're with that cop."

"You mean instead of your sister?" Trent snapped.
"Savannah and I are done!"

Who was Savannah? She crouched lower, thankful
Royd hadn't noticed her.

He spat out another swear word. His eyes rolled back
in his head. "So, you moved on to a cop? Come on,
Trent. I know you. You gotta do better than that."

Trent leaned forward. His voice grew deeper, more
dangerous. "My relationship with her is my business,
not yours!"

Shouts filled the air behind them. She looked back. It
looked like players and spectators were spilling from the
building. How long until somebody walked through the
parking lot enough to see Coach Henri pinning a man to
the ground on the other side of the van? Royd laughed so
hard he was spluttering. "O-oh, yeah, like I'm gonna believe you have a thing with Detective Brant. You think I
didn't do my homework before I paid her a visit? She's
fierce and she's totally clean. You're no way near at her
level. You don't have the smarts to either turn or play
somebody like her."

Trent's eyes grew dark. With one hand he shoved
Royd back into the ground. The other swung back and

his fist flew hard and fast at Royd so quickly the criminal's face went white in fear. Chloe's hand rose to her lips. But Trent pulled the punch, stopping mere inches from the criminal's nose.

"First you hurt her and then you insult me?" Trent snarled. "I'm gonna take pity on you because Savannah and I've got history. But you're gonna forget seeing me here. The payara deal is my business. You think Uncle's got you looped in on every deal he's got going?"

"You're nothing to Uncle—"

"Oh, yeah, then how come I'm still walking around alive with my heart still beating inside my body?"

Shouts were coming behind her now. Then she saw the smart, blue, uniformed form of Nicole and the male officer she'd been sitting with running toward them, a plain-clothed Butler two steps behind.

Looked like listening in was over and she was going to have to come out of her hiding place. Chloe ran around the van, holding out her badge. "We've got company!"

Trent leaned in toward Royd. "This isn't over. Keep your mouth shut." Then he grabbed Royd by the collar and yanked him to his feet. He thrust him at Chloe. "Cuff him. If anyone asks, he attacked you and I came to your defense. That's the truth. Now, I gotta go. Don't follow me. Don't call me. Don't try to come find me."

Her eyes searched the man standing in front of her. But Trent was gone and the hard man who stood in his place was nothing more than a stranger.

"But what about the hockey game?" Chloe said. Trent turned on his heels and strode off.

What about his cover?

"I'm sorry." He shook his head. "But I don't trust Royd to keep his mouth shut, and now that Royd knows I'm here, I can't be here anymore."

NINE

That was just Trent's cover talking, Chloe told herself. It had to be. Trent had seen a criminal from an old case and so he reassumed an old identity. He had to have said he was disappearing just for Royd's benefit. He didn't actually mean he was abandoning his Coach Henri identity, the Trillium players and moving on without her, right?

Yet, no matter how firmly she told herself that, something twisted in her chest as she watched Trent disappear around the side of the building, slinking like a wounded animal that didn't want to be seen. *Lord, what just happened? What do I do? I need a whole bunch of wisdom and clarity right now.* It was like Trent had transformed into a stranger right before her eyes and then abandoned her to handle the mess he'd left behind.

Butler had picked up his pace and overtaken the uniforms. She spun Royd around and pressed him against the van, feeling her brain go into autopilot as she recited the words she'd been saying to criminals for years. "I'm arresting you for assault with a weapon, assault of an officer and attempted kidnapping. It is my duty to inform you that you have the right to retain and instruct counsel without delay…"

Usually, this was the point of an arrest that whoever she was arresting pointed out the Canadian version of reading them their rights didn't match what they were used to hearing on American television. But Royd merely grunted. This almost certainly wasn't his first arrest on Canadian soil. Not to mention something had seemingly sapped his will to fight. Just who did Royd think Trent was? What side of him had he seen? She didn't know. She just had to trust that Trent had blown his cover to save her life and that he would fill her in as soon as he could. Chloe turned Royd around so that he faced her. "Do you understand?"

"Do you?" He scowled. "Word of advice, lady. Don't trust Trent. He uses women like you. He'll cut your heart out, chew it up and spit it in the gutter, just like he did to my sister, Savannah."

Another mention of Savannah and yet another reminder she didn't really know Trent at all. He'd told her he didn't have relationships.

"Detective Brant!" Butler arrived at her side with Nicole and the second uniformed officer now one step behind. "What do you think you're doing, arresting someone in my jurisdiction when you're off duty?"

"Sorry to interrupt your day off, Sir." She straightened. "This man is a member of the Wolfspiders. Goes by the name of Royd. I stepped outside and he jumped me, held a knife to my throat and demanded I tell him about payara. Thankfully, Coach Henri, was there to assist. You're right, I am off duty, so do go ahead and let Constable Docker take over the arrest. But when you question Royd, I want to sit in."

She stood back and let Nicole and the male officer who introduced himself as Constable Don Walleye, lead Royd toward a police cruiser.

"Where's Coach Henri now?" Butler frowned. "I told him we don't want civilians trying to do citizen's arrests on criminals."

"I honestly don't know where he is." Chloe crossed her arms and stared down her former training officer. The smell of alcohol surrounding him was even stronger now. "But don't start with me about people stepping out of bounds. You were my training officer. I know you're a sticker for the rules. But, like I told you, there's been gossip circling for weeks about the baggie-full of thousands of dollars' worth of payara pills found on these premises and the bungled investigation.

"Your division apparently failed to find out who's making the payara and now the Gulo Gulo Boys and the Wolfspiders have descended here, as well, trying to track that person down, too. You should be thankful it seems neither of them has succeeded. I'll cooperate with your investigation. But with all due respect, Sir, from what I'm hearing, your badge and reputation are on the line. Some random hockey coach tackling a thug who attacked his fiancée is the least of your worries."

Butler had gone white. His hands were shaking and she suspected he'd had more than one drink during the game. He started spluttering something about protocols and investigations taking time.

But she was done arguing. This whole situation was out of control. She'd come here hoping to help find the source of the drugs. Now the entire mess had spiraled so badly she didn't even know what she was supposed to do anymore. She took a deep breath and let it out slowly. Her job. She would do her job. She paused long enough to give her statement to Nicole's partner and then she turned and strode back to the sports center.

A small cluster of Trillium players, including Third Line, had gathered by the back doors. What were they thinking about all this? What could she possibly tell them? It was all fine and good of Trent to just snap from one cover identity to another on a dime, like the plastic doll with snap-on clothes she'd had as a child. What about the young people who'd spent three months building a relationship with Coach Henri only to have him disappear?

"Who was arrested, miss?" Aidan called.

"A Wolfspider gang member named Royd," she said, going for blunt honesty and deciding to give the "miss" a pass. "He tried to attack me. He didn't succeed. Now, who wants to tell me why you all stampeded out here when you're supposed to be in the middle of a hockey game?"

There was a long pause. Feet shuffled. Eyes darted right and left. Finally, Brandon blurted out, "Hodge charged out onto the ice during a face-off and sucker punched Johnny."

"Because somebody posted a picture of him kissing Poppy!" Hodge snapped.

"You shouldn't have been looking on social media during a game, anyway," Aidan said.

"I wasn't! But everybody else in the arena was and the next thing I know, like, six people were leaning over the back of the box shouting it at me."

"And I told you, that picture is a faaaaaaaake!" Poppy shouted the word like it had six syllables.

"Really?" Chloe looked around the crowd for Johnny. She didn't see him or any of the other Haliburton players. She turned to Poppy. "Who's behind it then?"

"I don't know!" Her voice rose to a wail but Chloe wasn't sure if she believed her.

"Hodge took payara before the game," Aidan added.

"No, I didn't!" Hodge spun on him.

Aidan didn't even blink. "I didn't say you did it on purpose!"

"Coach said somebody might've drugged him," Brandon explained. He held up a water bottle. "Coach said I should give you this and that Hodge should get a drug test."

Voices rose in a babble as multiple students started talking at once. Chloe raised a hand. "I got it. So a fight broke out and then you all collectively decided to run outside here at once because…?"

Her words trailed off. Voices fell just as quickly as they'd risen. Her question hung in the frozen air.

"I dunno," Milo said eventually. "People started yelling there was a fight outside and running for the exits. So I followed."

Crowd mentality. Super.

"Let me guess. None of you know who started the

stampede for the exits, either?" she asked. No answer. Right, so this was how it was going to be. Chloe pulled her badge out again and held it up, making sure everyone saw it. "As you guys all should know by now, I'm a detective with the Ontario Provincial Police. Most of my work is with the Special Victims Unit, which means it's not just my job to stop criminals. It's also my job to take care of people and protect them." She dropped her badge and crossed her arms. "So, I'm going to be straight with you. And I expect you to be straight with me.

"I know that a baggie of a new designer upper drug named payara was found in the locker room a few months ago. I know several of you were questioned about it. I also know the police didn't come up with enough evidence to arrest anyone, probably because you're all busy protecting each other. But that doesn't change the fact that someone in your community is cooking the stuff and somebody else is selling it. I wouldn't even be surprised if some of you have theories about who that could be." Her eyes fixed on Third Line. "I also wouldn't be surprised if it turns out more than one of you has tried it."

Nobody's eyes were meeting either hers now or even meeting each other's. Some scanned the snow falling from the dark sky above. Others scanned the edges of the parking lot. Hodge's face reddened as he stared directly at the ground.

"Now, maybe you think this isn't your problem and that it has nothing to do with you," she went on. "Maybe you only know rumors or don't want to get anybody else in trouble. Or you're worried about getting in trouble yourself. But yesterday three gang members took base-ball bats to your sports center and threatened your lives. Today, somebody from a different gang tried to kill me. That same big, creepy jerk broke into my house early this morning and attacked me."

Eyes grew wider. About half of them were meeting hers now. Poppy made a sound like a whimper. Lucy hugged herself. Aidan looked ready to punch someone.

"Frankly, I don't care what story you've been tell-ing yourself about why this isn't your problem. Your community is in danger and it probably isn't going to stop without your cooperation. So, here's what's going to happen. Right now, each and every one of you is going to take out your cell phone and add my phone number into your contacts. Text it to all your friends. Post it on the school message board. Give it to every-one you know.

"Then, go away and think long and hard about whether you really want criminals tearing up your community. When you decide the answer is no, text me everything you know. I'll find you a lawyer if you want one. I'll put you in touch with Victim Services or a social worker. You can block your number and text me anonymously, I don't care. Just give me what I need to protect you. Phones out. Now."

She waited as one by one the clump of students pulled out their phones. Then she recited her number slowly, watching them like a hawk. "Thank you. Now, unless any of you feel like confessing right now, I'm going to get out of this cold and get someone to process this water bottle and a drug test for Hodge. Any questions?"

Brandon raised his hand. "Where's Coach?"

"Honestly? I don't know." She waited while the youth dispersed slowly back into the building like shadows disappearing into the sun. Then she ushered Hodge over to Nicole's partner, Constable Walleye, handed him the water bottle and explained about the drug test. Thankfully, Hodge cooperated, although part of her suspected it was to get away from Poppy's attempts to pull him aside to talk.

There were no messages from Trent on her phone. She crossed the parking lot and walked around the front of the building. Trent's truck was gone.

She nearly screamed at the sky. So, Trent really had left, then. He'd dropped Coach Henri, switched covers and disappeared from her life without explaining what was happening or telling her why. She didn't even know why she was surprised.

A car honked at her twice as it drove out of the lot. Johnny was hanging out of a silver sports car. "Hey, Detective, I'm sorry for what happened earlier at the diner. George was being a fool. I saw Coach Henri pull out of here like his feet were on fire. Everything okay in paradise? Can I give you a ride anywhere?"

She nearly laughed in his face. From where she stood that flirtatious and cocky young man had caused more than enough trouble. "I'm good, thanks. Tell me, did you really kiss Poppy?"

"A gentleman doesn't kiss and tell!" Johnny slid back into the driver's seat.

Like he was a gentleman.

He lit a cigarette and puffed it out the window as he peeled out of the lot.

Now there was someone she'd have suspected of dealing drugs in a heartbeat, if she could figure out how Third Line fit into it. Trent was certain one of the four third-line players had hidden the payara in the locker room, and she didn't believe for a moment any of them would lie to police to protect Johnny, especially not considering how Hodge had pounded on him and apparently none of the players had tried to stop him. Had Trent been wrong about the timeline? Was Poppy really Trilly?

The taxi she had called took twenty minutes to arrive. Then it was an eighty-dollar fare back to her house. She spent it looking out the window and staring at the darkness rushing past. She never should've let herself kiss Trent. She never even should have let herself hold his hand. She never should've let Trent slide himself back into her life and infiltrate her heart.

Hers was the only vehicle in her driveway when she got home and her small hatchback was buried under a foot of snow. Her footsteps crunched on the cold, snowy ground. She undid both sets of locks on her front door and eased it open.

A tall form with broad shoulders sat silhouetted in her living room.

She yanked her service weapon and pointed it at him. "Hands up! Don't move!"

"Clo, it's me." Trent switched on the lamp. Her gaze fell on the short, buzzed hair and smooth, clean-cut face.

Gone was the softness of the beard and the gentle curl of his hair. Now shadows sharpened the lines of his jaw and traced along his cut shoulders and bulging biceps. A black T-shirt covered his chest. He leaned forward like an alpha animal. Torn jeans covered in motor oil stains gave way to the outline of a handgun near his ankle, just above a pair of steel-toed work boots. "Look, I'm sorry, but you have to trust me—"

"No, I don't." The gun held firm in her grasp. "I don't even know who you are anymore."

TEN

"Come on, Chloe. You can't possibly mean that," Trent said. Could she? He watched as Chloe holstered her weapon. Then she smacked on the switch to the main lights. Light flooded her living room.

"You broke into my house," she said.

"You left a spare key for the crime scene investigators." He stood. "I just picked it up from them, let myself in and locked the door behind me. They didn't find much but they'll have what they found analyzed in a few days—"

She cut him off. "Which hardly matters now that you clearly know who my attacker was."

Okay, she was angry. He'd expected as much. He bit his tongue and kept from pointing out that any evidence that Royd had broken into her home would still be helpful in getting a confession and conviction.

"Why didn't you tell me you knew him?"

"Because all I had was a suspicion." His jaw set. "There's more than one bald and bulked-up man out there with a spiderweb tattoo. Royd's full name is Roy

Denver. He's low-level Wolfspider fodder that Uncle throws at problems sometimes to see if he'll come back alive."

Trent wasn't even sure what he was doing in her living room. He had to drive two hours to Huntsville, find Uncle and get him to believe his side of the story before Royd managed to get word to them of what had happened.

As Chloe had slapped the handcuffs on Royd, he'd run back to his rented apartment, shaved off every last trace of Coach Henri and transformed into the version of himself he most hated looking at in the mirror. He'd been motoring down the highway, twenty minutes passed her house with Bobcaygeon in the rearview mirror, when he'd suddenly found himself turning his truck right back around and heading to Chloe's. Couldn't say for sure why. He just knew there was something inside him that kept kicking his brain like an old boot, telling him he needed to at least try to give her an explanation for his sudden shift in gears.

"I don't know what Royd's doing here," he added, "but I need to find out. Yesterday we had one gang involved in this payara mess. Now we have two—"

"So, you just took off?" Flames blazed in the green depths of her eyes.

"I came back!" he said.

"You blew your cover!"

"Because I had to." His arms crossed in front of his broad chest. "Royd and I have known each other for a long time. The moment I tried to help you he would've recognized me. But part of my arrangement with Uncle is that my family and girlfriend—if I ever had one—is off-limits. Either way, I was made. My cover was going to be blown. I couldn't just keep pretending to be a mild-mannered hockey coach.

"Yes, Royd was arrested and that will complicate my situation with the Wolfspiders. Royd'll probably get bail, and he'll most definitely get a phone call. Who knows how long it will be before he tells someone he saw me in Bobcaygeon and they figure out I was posing as a hockey coach. Or, for all I know, he might've even had someone else on the inside. I didn't come to town to coach hockey. I came here to stop the spread of payara. Sure, when this mission started my job was to get close to the third-line players. But the second I knew the Wolfspiders were involved, and that one of them would recognize me, then the mission changed. Don't you get that? I texted Eli, told him I had a personal emergency and needed him to take over the team, and also emailed my resignation to Trillium. It's done. All of it—Coach Henri, Trillium hockey, Third Line and the coach's cute fiancée—is over."

"Because that's how this works," she said. "You just snap your fingers and everything changes. Too bad for anyone who might care about Coach Henri or miss him."

"I'm an undercover cop. You know this. It's my job. It's never personal."

"Royd says you broke his sister Savannah's heart," Chloe said.

He winced. Yeah, he wasn't exactly proud of that. "Savannah has a crush on the person I pretend to be for my Wolfspider cover. Not on who I actually am. I promise I never intended to lead her on."

"He knew your real name, Trent. Not a cover name."

"Because, as we've covered, the best cover stories have a kernel of truth," he said.

Fact was, he'd been fourteen and still an uncontrollable ball of rage and pain about the death of his sister, when the students he occasionally hung with behind the gymnasium had introduced him to Uncle. Uncle had taken a liking to him and started giving him odd jobs to do, like picking up packages, looking out for cops and destroying things. Until, at seventeen, Trent had been arrested and scared straight by an understanding cop and gotten his life back on the straight and narrow. He'd never imagined his work as an undercover cop would mean using the shell of his teen life to concoct a new cover, based on a version of himself that he'd never really forgiven himself for.

"The Trent they know is a fixer," he added. "I randomly show up, after being away for months or even years, and use Uncle for information. He's a source and a gossip. He tells me what other gangs are doing because he knows I'll take care of it."

Chloe's eyebrows shot up.

"By getting them arrested! Sheesh, don't look at me like that! Uncle is a vital informant to our police operations and has absolutely no idea. Thanks to the information I've weaseled out of him, the RCMP have taken out human smuggling, child abuse rings, weapons trafficking and all sorts of other horrendous crimes that give cops nightmares. Even you've used information my cover has gotten from Uncle. When we first met, I was giving you intel I'd gotten from him about a Gulo operation."

But what he really wanted was to take Uncle down. Yes, Uncle was too clever about keeping his own hands clean, and Trent understood why his superiors believed an arrest shouldn't happen until they were confident the charges would stick. Not to mention that once Uncle believed Trent was no longer usable, he might come after Trent's family. But when Uncle finally slipped up, Trent wanted to arrest him personally.

"That's what's in jeopardy right now," he went on. "I don't know what Royd and the Wolfspiders have to do with payara, but it's a lead I can't afford to ignore. Uncle doesn't exactly trust me, and he won't be happy that I let you arrest Royd. I don't know what Uncle is going to think when he finds out that you and I have been telling everyone around town that we're engaged. Maybe he'll laugh it off like Royd did. But maybe he won't."

Or maybe, the Wolfspiders had an informant inside Bobcaygeon who'd seen them lock lips at the diner. "Either way, my roughing up a Wolfspider to save a cop looks really bad. In fact, it could destroy my Wolfspider cover for good. Not to mention it basically announces that I'm an obstacle in Uncle's way of getting his hands on payara. But I can probably manage to convince Uncle to tell me everything he knows about both the dealer and drug lab if I can spin it right."

Which he couldn't do as long as he stood around arguing in her living room. At least Chloe seemed to be listening now.

"Either I get the intel I need from Uncle tonight to find the payara dealer," he said, "or he discovers I've been playing him for years and he puts targets on both my back and yours. Those are the stakes. So, I've got to make tracks to get to Uncle first and spin him some story about how I've been romancing a pretty but foolish lady cop who doesn't realize I'm using her to get my hands on the drugs. No offense."

"None taken." A smirk turned at the corner of her lips that he didn't think he liked the look of. Then she turned and walked into the bedroom. The door slammed and locked behind her. "Give me thirty seconds. I'm coming with you."

"No, you're not!" He called through the door, "This is still my case, and there's absolutely no way that you're walking into a Wolfspider den with me."

"I'm going." It sounded like she was tossing the contents of her drawers and wardrobe on the floor. "My home stopped being safe when Royd broke in. Uncle could've sent someone else by now. Besides, someone needs to have your back."

"My back is just fine!" He paced to one side of the room and back again.

Help me, Lord, what am I doing here? Why did I even turn the truck around and come back? Why can't I walk away from this fight?

"The case might've changed, but we're partners." She pulled the door open so suddenly he tumbled to the floor, landing hard on one knee at her feet. He looked up and blinked.

Thick, knee-high combat boots encased her legs,

over a pair of leather motorcycle pants. She wore a black tunic dress over top, which fell all the way to her knees, with a studded leather bag that was half purse and half gun holster around her waist. A black leather motorcycle jacket completed the biker look but was almost swallowed up with the wild tumbling mass of thick red hair, now with unexpected shocks of pale blond extensions. Electric-blue eyes, framed with thick, artful dark lines met his.

"Stand up," she said. "And let's go. We can argue as we drive." Her lips were painted the same flaming red as her hair.

He stood slowly, opened his mouth and had to swallow twice before any words came out. "Who are you and what have you done with Chloe?"

"You think I've never walked into a room full of criminals who'd kill me as soon as they look at me?" She tossed her hair and it fell around her shoulders like a cape of flames. "Who do you think the Special Victims Unit sends in after those girls trapped in the kinds of nightmarish places you get intel from Uncle about? Detectives like me. I'm the one who walks through that door. I've been the one inside, providing surveillance, providing cover for the girls and giving the Emergency Response Unit the signal to burst in."

"The plan is to convince Uncle that I've been using you—"

"The plan is idiotic and going to get you killed." She cut him off. "Then, after they kill you, they'll send someone to kill me. You think Uncle is really going to believe that you're so smart and irresistible that you charmed a fierce and dedicated detective into spilling classified information without her knowledge. You really think you can sell that?"

Well, not to anyone who'd actually met her. But still.

"I don't have any other choice," he said.

"Yes, you do." Her hands snapped to her hips. "You keep trying to convince me that you're some expert on corrupt cops. We go in together, you introduce me as a bad apple and we tell them I only arrested Royd because there was a bunch of people coming my way and I needed to maintain my cover."

His eyes opened wider. "You expect me to walk into the middle of the Wolfspiders, right up to Uncle, with you on my arm, and tell him that the detective who Royd tried to rough up was just posing as my girlfriend because she's corrupt and wants a piece of my payara money?"

"Not quite." Her eyes fixed on his face through the blue contacts and he realized he'd know they were hers anywhere, no matter what color they were. "I'm going to walk in there and do what I don't believe you can. I'm going to convince Uncle that I sold out my badge, my honor and everything I believed in for you. We're going to tell them I'm your fiancée, and then I'm going to convince a roomful of killers that I've fallen head over heels for you, Trent. I'll make Uncle believe that he has nothing to fear from me and that he can still trust you. Because if I don't, you'll die."

ELEVEN

The Pit 11 Grill was a low, nondescript, squat structure that sat on a strip of highway outside Huntsville, Ontario. It was only about a twenty-minute drive from the warm family farmhouse where he'd grown up and would be going for Christmas dinner. But it felt like an entire world away. Yellow light seemed to drip in puddles from the sparse lampposts. The electric sign flickered blue through the thickly pelting snow. The parking lot was packed with battered Wolfspider vehicles.

Trent pulled to a stop at the far end of the lot. Then he felt his hand reach for Chloe's and squeeze it while he prayed. "God, help us in there. Keep us safe. Keep us smart. Keep us honest and honorable. Help us do what needs to be done, with as few people getting hurt in the process as possible."

"Amen," Chloe said.

He looked up through the windshield at the place that had harbored so many of his worst memories. He hated the Pit 11 Grill. He hated what he'd heard in there, what he'd seen in there and everything the dingy restaurant represented. A person like Chloe didn't belong in a place like that. Yes, as a cop she'd walked bravely into even uglier places for the sake of justice and mercy. But the dirt of what Pit 11 stood for was like a stain on his heart. She deserved better than to be led by a man like him into a place like that.

"Any last words?" she asked.

He winced. He wished she hadn't put it like that. He looked down at her slender gloved hand enclosed in his and felt the lump of the engagement ring beneath the leather. He wanted to tell her that the story of his life had some ugly chapters he hoped she'd never read and that his heart had some dark places he hoped she never saw. He wanted to tell her that as grateful as he was that he'd turned his life around, he wished there was a way to scour every corner of his past so that he'd never even needed that forgiveness God had offered him. "If you sense your life is in danger, I want you to get yourself out of there, okay? Don't hesitate. Don't look back. Got it?"

"Got it." She pulled her hand from his. "But for the record, if anyone pulls a gun on you and threatens to kill you, I'm shooting them first. Even if it's Uncle."

He chuckled. "Deal. You can shoot only if he tries to kill me. But only then."

As they walked toward the building, he could feel his shoulders roll back, his chest puff out and his gait slow to a cocky saunter. They reached the door and he felt Chloe's left arm drop possessively around his shoulders, as confident and smooth as if it belonged there. His arm slid around her waist. Her lips brushed his cheek and an odd warmth filled his core as he realized that for the very first time, when he stepped through those doors, he wouldn't feel utterly alone.

They stepped over the threshold into a dark space filled with wobbly round tables and even wobblier patrons. The air stunk of alcohol spilled long ago. Faces he recognized and strangers whose types he knew all too well cut him furtive glances. His eyes narrowed and locked on the white-bearded, barrel-chested man nursing something in an unmarked bottle at the counter.

Uncle glanced up.

Trent counted at least two enforcers flanking him—a tall one to his left and a shorter but heavily armed one to his right. Trent kept his eyes locked on his target and strode toward him with the swagger of a man who knew every crack in the counter and the kinds of deals that had been made over them.

He made it six steps from the place where Uncle sat before the taller enforcer leaped in front of him and lobbed a sucker punch at Trent's jaw, knocking him clear out from under Chloe's arm. Trent took the blow and staggered back. Then he reared forward, grabbed the enforcer by the throat and shoved him hard against the counter. Trent glanced at Uncle. "What kind of welcome is this for an old friend?"

Uncle snorted. "What kind of old friend disappears for months and drops off the grid?"

"The kind who's been busy and had things to do." Trent stepped back. The enforcer hesitated. Uncle nodded at him. The enforcer slunk to the end of the counter and glowered at him like a guard dog. Trent reached for Chloe's hand and pulled her over to stand beside him.

"Heard you'd tried going straight again," Uncle said. He cast his eyes over Chloe then turned back to Trent. "Let me guess. You ran out of money and so you're back asking for work."

"I'm here to find out why you sent Royd to rough up my woman!" Trent swept Chloe's hair back off her throat and showed the dark bruises Royd's fingers had left on her skin. He let her hair fall. "Babe, take off your gloves."

She did. Trent held up her left hand and showed Uncle the bruises on her wrist just long enough to make sure he also saw the engagement ring on her hand.

"I don't know what Royd's got against your woman." Uncle shrugged. "Maybe Savannah's mad you moved on, so she put him up to it."

"You mean Royd just decided to try to rough up and kidnap a cop all on his own?" Trent's voice rose.

The room froze. Uncle turned. His face went white. "You brought a cop into my business?"

"I brought my woman into your restaurant, because you and I have a history and she asked to meet you. She's been poking around Bobcaygeon trying to find out how to get her hands on payara. She took out a group of Gulos because they were after the same thing. Then you send Royd after her? You have any idea who this woman is? Or how solid her reputation is? She's connected. She's fierce. She could've been a major asset to you, for the right price. She could've helped you out and worked with you to get you whatever you needed. Instead you sent Royd to take her on." Trent shook his head.

"You must be Detective Brant." Uncle stretched a large calloused hand toward Chloe.

She took his hand and shook it. "Call me Chloe."

"My apologies, Chloe. I had no idea you and Trent were an item, or that you'd be interested in doing business. You two set a date to get hitched?"

"Not yet." Chloe smiled. It was a look full of confidence and courage, and incredibly attractive. "Trent's pretty stubborn when he wants to be."

Uncle laughed. Trent couldn't believe it. Chloe was actually charming the head of the Wolfspiders. "Remind him that a married woman can't be forced to testify against her husband in court, but a girlfriend can."

She grinned wider, then shot Trent a glance that made him suddenly realize just how helpless he'd be if she ever really did turn her will against him. "Will do."

"Give me a moment with your boy?" Uncle gestured to the back of the room. "He and I have some business to discuss alone. Then you and I can sit down and see about making a deal."

The hair rose suddenly on the back of Trent's neck. No, this wasn't the plan. But Chloe had already slipped from his side and brushed her lips against his cheek, filling his senses with the scent of her skin. "No problem. It was a long drive and I could use some freshening up. Don't make any decisions without me."

She turned and headed toward the back. All eyes in the room watched her go.

"You've got it bad," Uncle said. "How do you know she's not planning on arresting you?"

Trent snickered. "She wouldn't. I can trust her."

"How would you know?" Uncle turned back to his drink. "You're head over heels for that chick. Not to mention she's way out of your league. A woman like that doesn't take up with a guy like you without a really good reason."

Trent held his tongue. He knew Chloe was far better than a man like him deserved. He didn't need a criminal like Uncle reminding him of that. *One day, Lord, I will get a warrant to arrest Uncle and take down the Wolfspiders for good. One day, I will close this chapter of my life for good and never use this cover again.*

"So what does your family think of her?" Uncle raised an eyebrow. "You going to pop by with her for a visit while you're in town?"

"Wasn't planning on it." Trent's jaw clenched. He didn't even want to imagine how that would go down. They'd probably love her. "But I'm not here to talk about her. I'm here to talk about payara."

"Oh, but I think the bigger issue is family, don't you?" There was a mocking tone in the old man's voice, but the hint of something evil glinted in his eye. "I saw your dad just recently."

Trent felt his face go pale. His father? His parents were in their sixties and the nicest, most honest, caring and down-to-earth people anyone would ever want to meet. Not to mention, their farm was less than half an hour's drive away. Uncle had never made a move against his family, and Trent knew he never would as long as he thought Trent was useful to his operation. But Trent had tried to warn his folks and brothers, more than once, that when the day finally came that he took Uncle down they should sell the farm and move out of Wolfspider territory. He just had to pray they would. His eyes narrowed. "What are you playing at?"

"Nothing," Uncle said. "I happened to be in the Huntsville cemetery and saw him laying flowers on your sister's grave."

Anger built like heat at the back of Trent's neck. Was this Uncle's way of tightening his stranglehold on the man Trent pretended to be when he was undercover? *Lord, I do this job to save lives and protect the innocent. Please, don't let one more person I love get hurt because of me.* "Are you threatening my family? We had an arrangement, Uncle. The day I became a Wolfspider, you promised my family would be off-limits."

Uncle had to know that if he ever went after his family, Trent would slap the cuffs on him.

"I'm just making friendly conversation." Uncle slapped his empty bottle down on the counter and another one appeared. "When I sent Royd to see what he could about getting me into payara production, I knew that the Gulos had staged a failed attempt to get their hands on it. I knew there was a cop involved. I didn't know it had anything to do with you, or that you were even there. If I had, I'd have given you the opportunity to handle it. But since you didn't, I've now got a race on my hand to see which one of you can deliver first."

He took a long sip from the new bottle then fixed his eyes on Trent. "Because, make no mistake, I am taking over the payara operation, one way or another. I am getting hold of that lab and convincing whoever's working the drug to come work for me. Our arrangement still stands. You stay out of my business, I'll stay out of yours. But if you try to double-cross me, or take that payara distribution for yourself, you just might have to get used to visiting a whole row of new headstones in the family plot, starting with that pretty cop you think you're going to marry."

Chloe leaned back against the cracked counter in the surprisingly large but dingy women's washroom and peered through a crack in the door. Something was wrong. Trent's shoulders were hunched like a protective lion. Whatever Uncle was saying had angered him. She watched as the enforcer who'd sucker punched Trent by way of a welcome left his post at the end of the counter and shifted closer to Trent and Uncle. Another enforcer had materialized behind them. She took a deep breath and reminded herself that Trent knew exactly what he was doing and if he needed her, he'd find a way to let her know. She didn't know which was worse—throwing off a seasoned detective in the middle of the undercover interrogation of a gang leader, or staying back, when every beat in her chest told her he needed her by her side? She knew the answer. She was going out there.

The door flew inward. A woman stood in the doorway, a snarl on her lips and her hands on her hips. She was brunette and curvy, with the kind of face classically considered quite beautiful and a stance that implied she thought Chloe had invaded her territory.

"Excuse me," Chloe said. To her surprise, the woman stepped out of the way to let her pass. But as Chloe's hand brushed the door frame, the brunette slammed it shut again so quickly and violently that the speed of Chloe's reflexive move to leap back was the only thing that kept her from having her fingers broken. The brunette closed the door behind them. Chloe felt her green eyes narrow behind their blue contacts. "Do we have a problem?"

The attractive brunette snorted. "You're not welcome here. Get out before I hurt you."

Chloe planted her feet. "Let me guess, you're Savannah? I hear you and my man have history."

Savannah's eyes widened, just long enough to let Chloe know she'd hit her mark. Chloe shook her head. Savannah was a distraction. Nothing more. Chloe pitied her, even knowing what Trent's cover had done to her feelings. Maybe they had that much in common.

"You're the cop who thinks she's going to marry Trent," Savannah said. Seemed news traveled fast. "Let me guess, you think you're in love with him?"

Yes was the word Chloe knew her cover required her to say. During the drive she'd even rehearsed in her head how to say that she had feelings for Trent. Yet, as she stood there, in the dingy washroom of a run-down restaurant that served as the front for a gang operation, she couldn't do it. Whatever it was she felt for Trent, it cut way too deep just to be blurted out meaninglessly on an undercover mission. "Well, we're getting hitched."

"No, you're not," Savannah said. "There's no way

Trent Henry's ever marrying anyone. If you think he is, you don't really know him."

Chloe almost laughed. This woman's jealousy was ridiculous. "And you do?"

An unsettling confidence flashed in the depths of Savannah's eyes. "I've known Trent since the second grade."

The words hit Chloe's ears like a thunderclap. Her knees almost buckled. "You're lying."

"Oh, no. Trent was my high school crush!" Now it was Savannah's turn to laugh. "He didn't tell you, did he? We've been on and off since we were teens. We used to go around Huntsville hot-wiring cars and going on joyrides. Who do you think introduced him to Uncle and got him in with the Wolfspiders? My brother, Royd, did. Who do you think he called when being a cop got old and he wanted back in? Me."

Pieces of the picture that was Trent turned and clicked into place in her mind. No wonder he'd been able to return to the Wolfspider cover more than once. No wonder Royd knew his real name. Trent had gone undercover with a deadly gang, time and again, by playing a corrupt and twisted version of his younger self. Her eyes dragged her gaze back to the closed door that blocked Trent from her view. Why hadn't he told her? She might not know his whole story or the cover roles he played, but she knew the man he was on the inside.

"You're right," Chloe said. "I haven't known Trent as long as you have. I don't know his history or everything he's done. But I know his heart. That's good enough for me." It was high time she got back out there and by his side. "Now, are you going to step aside and let me out? Or am I going to have to move you?"

"You can't rescue him," Savannah said. "The best you can do is cut your losses and run. I know about Royd's arrest. I know Trent chased him down and held him for you."

"How?" A chill spread through Chloe's limbs.

"Royd has friends. One of them already called me. My brother is moving up in the world. Royd knows who's selling the payara. It's only a matter of time before he gets him to cut a deal for Uncle."

Savannah was still smirking. She clearly didn't understand the importance of what she'd just said or that she was telling Chloe something she didn't already know. But Chloe's blood ran cold. Uncle already knew who was selling the payara. That meant Uncle didn't need Trent for anything. Uncle was just lying to Trent for his amusement or to find out what the police knew. Trent had walked right into a trap and he didn't know it.

Chloe shoved Savannah aside, yanked the door open and strode back into the dining room. Her fingers snapped. "Trent! Honey! Toss me the keys. We're leaving! Now!"

Her voice rang like a bell through the crowded room. Trent frowned. Then he grabbed his keys from his pocket and pitched them to her. She caught them one-handed.

"Go do what you need to do," he said. "I'll join you in a bit."

"No, you're coming with me now!" Her hands were planted on her hips. Was it her imagination or were the men closing in tighter around them? "I've just been talking to Savannah and she's been filling me in on your past. You come now or you can forget about marrying me."

Trent glanced at Uncle and shrugged. Then he cut his eyes over her shoulder. Savannah had followed her. He groaned. "Look, whatever Savannah said to you, it doesn't matter. Just ignore her."

He meant it. She could read that much in his eyes. He thought she was making a mistake.

"Trent, trust me, if you don't come talk with me, you're an idiot." Glimmers of a warning pushed its way through her words, begging to be heard. She strode over to him, weaving her way through the gang members that stood around him like a pack of animals waiting to strike. She stopped, her toes inches away from his. They were so close that all she had to do was lean forward and their lips would be touching. "I'm not your sidekick. I'm not your woman. I'm your equal. And I'm telling you, I want to go talk."

"Is there a problem, Trent?" Uncle raised an eyebrow.

She took a step back and almost felt the wall of gang members hemming them in. *Help me, Lord. I can't stop the danger. And Trent's too confident in the strength of his cover to see it's about to self-destruct around him.* She grit her teeth. Well, if they were going down, then she was going down swinging.

"I didn't come here to be treated like this!" Chloe yanked the ring off her finger and flung it at him. To her surprise, Trent leaped off the stool and scrambled for it. She swung back toward Savannah. "Why didn't you tell me you and Savannah had a history? I thought I knew you. But I don't and I never will. Because you're so determined to shut people out, you hurt everyone who cares about you and wreck everything you touch. And I'm done with it."

Chloe spun around so quickly that her flailing arm made contact with Savannah's jaw and knocked her back a foot. No one watching would've believed it was on purpose.

But that hardly mattered. The profanity that escaped Savannah's lips was primal. The blow she leveled across Chloe's cheek was even more so. Then Savannah leaped at her, yanking out Chloe's clipped-in hair extensions and trying to dig her nails into Chloe's face. Chloe reared back, tossing Savannah into the nearest enforcer. Before she could take another step, she felt Trent's arms around her waist, lifting her feet off the ground.

"What are you playing at?" Trent snapped. "You actually trying to start a fight?"

He pulled her backward toward the door. His voice rose. "Uncle, I'm sorry, just give me a minute."

He kicked the door open and they tumbled outside. Trent dropped her into the snow. Frustration filled his gaze. She looked back over his shoulder. Uncle was standing. A crowd of Wolfspiders was watching them. She threw her arms around Trent's neck and hugged him, feeling for that familiar space in his shoulder that meant safety. But his arms weren't about to yield.

"Chloe, my past with Savannah is none of your business—"

"Royd has already found out who the payara dealer

is and has been negotiating with him. He has a contact on the inside in Bobcaygeon who called Savannah tonight. I don't know if Uncle knows that Royd's already found the dealer. If he does, it means Uncle knows he doesn't need you and we've walked into a trap. If he doesn't, you don't want to be sitting there making him promises when he finds out the truth."

Trent pulled back. His eyes met hers. He believed her and he was sorry. She could see both truths clearly in a single glance. That was all she needed. Then he leaned forward and kissed her on the forehead and whispered, "We gotta run."

She turned and ran for the truck, knowing without a moment's hesitation that Trent would be right behind her. She heard voices shouting and the Wolfspiders pouring through the door. Then she heard Trent grunt as an enforcer leaped on him from behind. She looked back. Trent was down on his knees, struggling as the large man tried to choke him. Trent reared back and shook him off. An agonizing pop filled the air. Trent howled in agony. He'd dislocated his shoulder. "Trent!"

"Don't stop!" He struggled to his feet. "I'm right behind you!"

She reached the truck first and yanked the passenger door open for Trent. Within seconds he was inside. She slammed the door and sprinted for the driver's side, wiping as much snow off the back window as she could with the palm of her hand. The keys slid into the ignition. The engine turned over. Her eyes slid to the rearview mirror. Wolfspiders were jumping into vehicles. She glanced at Trent.

"Don't worry," she said, "we'll get you to a hospital and they'll pop your shoulder back in."

Engines roared behind them. She fired back, barely missing a van, then yanked the steering wheel and gunned the truck onto the narrow country road. The windshield wipers worked hard and fast against the falling snow.

"They're not going to let us go that easily," Trent said. "Uncle's going to get them to run us off the road."

"I didn't hear him say that." Her fingers tightened on the wheel.

"He doesn't need to," Trent said. "Nobody just gets up and walks out on a conversation with Uncle without paying a price for it. Car crashes are one of the ways Uncle deals with people and why I've never been able to pin a murder or an assault on him. He orders people to drive someone off the road and then gets them to ditch the vehicle, leaving him untouchable."

"He's not untouchable." She looked up. The bright glare of high beams filled the rearview mirror. "We're going to get out of this, and you're going to be the one to eventually take him down."

A vehicle bumped them hard from behind. Her body slammed against the seat belt. Trent shouted out in agony. His face was paler than she'd ever seen it before. How many jolts could his body take before he passed out from the pain? A white van was riding her back bumper. A large red truck was coming up on her left. Trees and a frozen lake lay to her right. The van bumped them again. The truck swerved. She prayed hard, struggling with the steering wheel and fighting to keep them on the road.

Trent dropped his cell phone onto his lap. "Call Jacob."

From Criminal Investigations? "I'll call 9-1-1."

"No!" Trent's shout echoed through the cab. "Call Jacob! Tell him everything. He knows who you are. He knows I'm undercover. He'll know what to do."

"But—"

"He's my brother!"

"You have a brother?"

"I have three. I grew up on a farm not twenty minutes from here. Tell my family that I'm sorry."

Sorry for what? The red truck sideswiped them so hard she felt the steering wheel yanked from her grasp. They spun. She grabbed for the wheel. But it was too late. The road disappeared from under them. She was thrown against the door as Trent's truck began to roll, tumbling down the hill.

Help us, Lord!

They were going to crash.

TWELVE

Darkness swept over Trent in waves, with fractured thoughts slipping through the gaps of unconsciousness. The truck was rolling. Prayers slipped like screams through Chloe's lips. They were upside down. Right-side up. Sideways. Then they stopped. Pain smashed into his body like a sledgehammer. He passed out.

Gunshots yanked his mind back to consciousness. Chloe had crawled out of the vehicle and was firing her weapon in the direction of the road.

"Stay back! You come one step closer and I'm going to shoot!" A long, tense silence fell as he lay there in the vehicle, helpless as she faced down the criminals who had run them off the road.

Suddenly he felt Chloe's strong, determined hands pulling his body from the wreckage and out into the snow. Coldness pressed against his back and flakes were falling on his face.

"They're gone," she said. "A red truck without legible plates ran us off the road. An enforcer from the grill got out and doubled-checked that we'd really crashed. I fired at him. He took off."

So today wasn't the day he was going to die. Uncle had ordered his enforcers to run Trent off the road as a punishment or warning, but not told them to finish the job. It wasn't unusual for Uncle to "warn" someone several times before finally coming to kill them. It was one of the ways he kept people in line and terrified of him. He should probably be thankful this was the first beating Uncle had ever meted out on him. Seemed whatever business Uncle had with him, he wasn't through with him yet.

He heard Chloe on the phone with Jacob, telling him where they were and what was happening. *Thank You, God.* Jacob would know what to do. But how could Trent ever forgive himself for dragging Chloe into danger?

He felt the warmth of Chloe curling her body against his chest and pulling an emergency blanket over them both. He groaned.

"You're not allowed to die, Trent! You hear me?" Her stern voice cut through the darkness and pain filling his mind. "You're going to stay that same stubborn man I care about who's too pigheaded to die. You got that? You're staying alive! I need you and I don't want to live without you. You hear me?"

I hear you, Chloe. I'm here. I'm so sorry I didn't listen sooner.

Words filled his mind, but before he could get his mouth to work, unconsciousness swept over him again. Then he heard more voices. Deep, strong, familiar voices were shouting his name and filling his chest with hope. A pair of large hands felt for a pulse.

"Yeah, he's alive," a male voice said. It was Jacob, his older brother. "Hang on, bro. Max's going to give you something for the pain."

Max? His younger brother, the paramedic?

Hey, guys, I'm fine. This darkness just keeps taking over and I keep passing out.

"If you want pancakes, you're going to have to wake up eventually," Jacob said.

Trent opened his eyes. He was lying on a bed. There was a blanket draped over him. Bright morning sunshine streamed through a window to his right. His eyes focused slowly as shapes swam before him. A row of plastic dinosaurs growled and snarled down at him from a shelf at the end of the bed. He groaned and leaned back against the pillow. He was home. He was lying in his very own childhood bed at the Henry family farmhouse.

"Look, I'm just warning you, as your big brother," Jacob added, "it's Christmas Eve brunch and Mom's pulled out all the stops. So the fact that you were run off the road by an evil, criminal gang isn't going to keep us from eating all the good stuff and leaving you with nothing but cereal."

He glanced sideways. A tall man, with broad shoulders and chestnut hair, was sitting on a single bed on the opposite side of the bedroom that had been way too small for them even as kids.

"I'm saying we split his pancakes and just don't tell

him." A second voice dragged his attention to the doorway. Max's strong bulk leaned against the frame, his short black hair a mass of curls.

"Nobody eats my pancakes," Trent muttered. He tried to roll over onto to his side and almost yelped in pain as his shoulder hit the mattress. There was a sling wrapped around his arm and shoulder. No doubt his paramedic brother's doing. "What's going on? What am I doing here?"

"Steady there, buddy," Max said. "You have a dislocated shoulder and a nasty concussion." He crossed the floor in two long strides, crouched beside his brother's bed and helped him sit. Then he glanced across the room at Jacob. "If I'd known the threat of stealing his pancakes was going to wake him up, I'd have done it twenty minutes ago."

"No, you wouldn't. You'd have gone ahead and eaten them before he could stop you." Jacob chuckled then leaned forward, resting his elbows on his knees. "We got there less than twenty minutes after the truck crashed. Max and I dragged you up the hill, took you home and got you patched up. Max and Nick popped your shoulder back in. You were conscious. But Max warned us you might not remember much. You've been asleep for about nine hours."

"Last thing I remember, I was in the truck," Trent said as his mind filed the pieces back into order. "We were being chased by some vehicles. I was in pain. I told Chloe—" He leaped to his feet so quickly his head swam and his knees buckled. "Where's Chloe?"

"Downstairs in the kitchen having breakfast with

the family." Max caught him by his good arm before he crumpled to the ground.

"Is she okay?" Trent asked. "Is she hurt? Was she injured?"

"She's fine." Max firmly guided him back down to the bed. "A few bruises from the crash. But in way better shape than you. You need to take it easy. You're going to want to avoid any strenuous physical activity for the next few days. Nothing involving your shoulder for at least two weeks."

He nearly groaned in frustration. This was no time for him to be out of commission. Trent glanced at Jacob. "How is Chloe, really?"

Jacob glanced at Max. Neither of them spoke for a beat. Then Jacob said, "Max, why don't you go get some pancakes and tell the rest of the fam that Trent's awake? We'll join you in a moment."

Max nodded and headed down the stairs, with a parting reminder not to mess with the shoulder sling.

Jacob turned to Trent. "Chloe's fine. Really. She's strong and resilient. But as you can imagine, she's got a lot of questions. I take it you never told her about any of us."

No, he hadn't. Now Chloe was sitting in his parents' kitchen, on Christmas Eve, eating pancakes with his parents and his two younger brothers. "I take it she knows everything now?"

"No, we dragged her to a houseful of strangers, put her to bed on the foldout in the den and fed her breakfast without telling her that we were your family." Jacob laughed. Trent didn't. "Of course she knows who we are. She's now met all of us. She knows this is the farm-house where you grew up. That's where things are at. But we respect your privacy, so the rest is up to you."

Trent winced. "So, you didn't tell her about Faith?"

The smile faded from Jacob's face. "We figured that was your story to tell."

There was a more than ten-year gap between the old-est and youngest of the Henry brothers. Max had just been a toddler when Faith had died. Nick hadn't even been born yet. But Jacob had been fourteen when their sister had been killed. He'd been the one standing out-side when Trent had sauntered home, waiting to explain why there were cop cars parked on the lawn, and the crying from the house was so loud he could hear it from the driveway. The death of their sister was a shared but mostly silent bond between them, even as they each pursued a career in law enforcement.

"Thank you." It was a conversation he knew he needed to have with Chloe. If he was honest with him-self, it was the one topic that every other conversation he'd ever avoided having with her had come down to. He'd once had a younger sister. She'd been murdered by a killer who'd never been caught. He'd blamed himself.

"Chloe saved your life, you know." Jacob's voice cut through Trent's thoughts. "If she hadn't steered the truck clear of the trees before the crash, or dragged you out of the truck, or kept you warm until we got there, or called me…"

Or caused a scene to get him out of the Pit when he was too stubborn to listen.

"I'd be dead twice over," Trent said. "I know. She's

a spectacular cop and I owe her my life. Did she or you file a police report?"

"Against Uncle and the Wolfspiders, no. She informed the higher-ups, of course. But she said whether actual charges are pressed is your call. She said you guys never heard Uncle give the order to cause the accident and that when she challenged the criminal who'd run you off the road, he just turned and walked away. My guess, and hers, is that the vehicle's already been ditched by now and they staged it to look like an accident. It's your investigation and taking down the Wolfspiders is your deal."

That was one way of putting it.

"It was a warning," he said. "If Uncle wanted to kill us, we'd be dead by now. He's probably still hoping he can use me." Trent stood. So did Jacob. Was it his imagination or had the room shrunk even more since they were kids? They were both practically hitting their heads on the slanted ceiling. "Chloe probably thinks I've acted like an idiot."

"Well, maybe you have," Jacob said. He smiled.

"Maybe." Trent chuckled and ran his hand over his jaw. The stubble he'd shaved off yesterday was already starting to grow back. "Chloe doesn't let me get away with anything."

Then the smile faded from his face. "I've been undercover with the Wolfspiders for years, and this is the first time Uncle has turned against me. I can't assume it'll be the last. Knowing him, he'll probably lay low for a bit and wait to see what my next move is. Hopefully the fact that I'm going to disappear and fall off the map again when I head to the diamond mine will be enough to make him think he's scared me into hiding. If he still truly believes I'm dirty, he'll think I'm more use to him alive. He won't make a big move against the family if he thinks he can still use me. But when I finally do take him down, it will put a target on the backs of everyone I love."

His brother nodded. "We'll discuss it with the family. I'll try to convince the folks to take a holiday somewhere warm for a few weeks while we wait to see how this is all going to play out. Then maybe I should move home for a bit to keep an eye on the folks while you're away."

"Maybe," Trent said. *Lord, am I overreacting? Was Uncle just meting out a beating on me to remind me who's in charge? Or does last night mean everything's changed in my game of cat and mouse with Uncle, and he'll come after me again?*

Jacob went downstairs, leaving Trent to get dressed in a borrowed pair of jeans and a plaid shirt. Of the four Henry boys, only the youngest, Nick, still lived at home, and even then only between stints of military service. But the four bachelor brothers always returned home for Christmas. He never imagined he'd be the first one to bring a woman home for the holidays, even if he hadn't done it on purpose.

His feet walked slowly down the wooden stairs and crossed through the living room. A fire crackled in the redbrick hearth, filling the space with warmth. A real and towering Christmas tree stretched up to the ceiling. The sound of laughter and the smell of bacon floated toward him. He paused in the doorway. Mom and Dad, Jacob, Max and Nick all sat around the old kitchen table passing plates of food, eating and talking. And there, in the middle of it all, sat Chloe, clad in one of his old gray sweatshirts and a pair of his jeans from high school days, when he was still all stringy limbs and before he'd put on any bulk.

He watched as she laughed and smiled, bantered with his family about her plans to spend Christmas dinner with her sister's family and accepted the bacon Max dumped on her plate before drizzling a dose of his mother's maple syrup over it. Chloe fit with his family, somehow. She belonged there, in that happy mass of Henry family breakfast, in a way he was never sure he had.

"Trent! Sit! Eat!" His father's voice boomed through the kitchen. Trent felt all faces turn. But no sooner had Chloe's eyes met his than she looked back down at her plate again. His father crossed the room toward him. "Food's getting cold. I was just about to throw some extra bacon on."

"Dad, Mom, guys, I'm sorry to cause you all so much trouble. We need to talk about what last night could mean, for all of us."

His dad's large, callused hand landed on his shoulder.

"I know." His dad's voice dropped. "Jacob's already briefed us. He's called someone from Victim Services who can come brief us later, and we will talk more. In the meantime, stop blaming yourself for things out of your control. Sit. Eat. Talk to your family. It's Christmas Eve." He steered him toward the seat beside Chloe, even as Nick rose to vacate it and pull up a chair on the other side of the table. "You're home now."

Home. In Dad's way of thinking that meant the place where some things didn't have to be said and long explanations didn't have to be given, because being sorry was enough to be forgiven, and forgiveness was all that mattered. But what happened when someone did something bigger than a mere apology could cover? How did a person just accept forgiveness, drop their baggage at the door and take a seat at the table?

Sure, he'd physically stepped through the door and joined the family, dozens and dozens of times, acting like he was one of them. But somehow it had never been enough to fully remove that invisible barrier he'd felt spring up and block off his heart from theirs in the terrible moment he'd learned that Faith had died.

No matter how many times he'd told them he was sorry for not keeping her safe and they'd assured him he was forgiven.

No matter how many times his father told him he was home.

His father's hand was still resting kindly on his shoulder. Trent sat beside Chloe and said sheepish hellos around the table, thanking them all for what they'd done last night. He took the food his family passed him and the coffee Jacob poured into his cup. His good shoulder brushed against Chloe's.

"I'm sorry," he said. "This isn't how I wanted you to meet my family."

"They're really rather wonderful." She smiled. But her gaze seemed to sweep in everyone but him.

"Are you okay?" he asked. Was she hurt? Was she angry or disappointed in him? Were they still okay?

"I'm a little sore," she said. Her eyes were green again, without the colored contacts she'd worn the night before. "As I gather Jacob told you, I called the powers that be and filled them in on what happened last night and the state of our investigation. Apparently the Wi-Fi went down in the night, so I've only been able to use your family's landline. Your brother Nick is hoping to get the Wi-Fi back right after breakfast."

She smiled and yet her eyes stayed silent. As if that secret and unspoken connection they shared—the one that enabled them to read each other's thoughts in a glance—was gone. She held up her mug toward Jacob for a refill of fresh coffee.

"Fresh cream and maple syrup, right?" Max asked.

"Oh, absolutely." She reached out her hands as they were passed down the table to her.

Trent watched as she poured both into her coffee and stirred it slowly, turning it from her usual plain black to the color of caramel that, to her, meant comfort and home.

Conversation flowed again around the table like an invisible current of warmth and happiness, sweeping Chloe up along with it and carrying her along. As breakfast finished, he stood and reached to help clear the dishes. But his mother waved him down. "Don't worry about it, Trent. We've got more than enough hands. Why don't you go show Chloe the barn?"

The barn. In other words, she was suggesting he

take Chloe to the one place on the family farm where he used to go to deal with the loss of his sister, Faith.

It was a conversation he and Chloe needed to have, and should have probably had long before this moment. Now, with everything crashing around him, could he really afford the time to open his heart to Chloe?

"Don't worry," Jacob said softly, as if reading his mind. "Whatever we do next, it can wait twenty minutes. Nick's busy working on the phones. I'm going to sit Mom and Dad down to talk about that vacation we talked about. There's only one road into the farm and the barn's close. You'll be in sight lines of the farmhouse the entire time. I've got things covered."

Right. But still, the sooner he left the farm the safer his family would be.

He glanced at Chloe. She nodded. "Sounds good to me."

He found his coat hanging on his childhood hook by the back door and his boots in the cubby with his name on it. Chloe helped him zip it up over the sling. They pushed through the back door. Bright sunshine met his eyes, filtering through thick flakes that danced in incongruously from pale clouds to the north. Snow lay thick and white in pure unbroken sheets at their feet, spreading out to the horizon.

Trent and Chloe walked, in silence, their footsteps crunching in the snow, past the frozen pond and toward the barn. His eyes searched her face as they walked. But her features were so emotionless it was like she was carved from ice.

"I'll be honest, Chloe," he said. "So much has happened in the past twenty-four hours that I literally don't have a clue what to say right now. Two days ago, I was a hockey coach, facing down the end of my investigation into which of four young men in Third Line had a connection into a dangerous new designer drug. It was supposed to be a quick and simple assignment.

"All I had to do was find out who was making and selling the stuff then I could move on to my next investigation. But then the Gulos attacked the sports center and threatened Third Line. You sprung to their rescue and mine.

"Then you were attacked, a potential informant reached out, we went undercover together, Royd attacked again and suddenly I discovered the so-called simple case I was working on was actually linked to the biggest, meanest, nastiest gang I knew and their leader, Uncle. It's like an onion that keeps having layer after layer and each one is worse the deeper it goes. Then the Wolfspiders drove us off the road and you saved my life, called my brother and brought me home."

Chloe stopped walking. He stopped, too, and she turned toward him. And for the first time since the moment they'd met, he saw an emotion in the depths of her eyes he'd never seen directed at him before. She was angry and something about that knocked him back further than a physical blow ever could. "Why are you angry?"

"I never said I was angry—"

"You didn't have to. Chloe, it's me. I can usually read your face. Just like you can usually read mine."

She shook her head, like she was trying and failing

to shake the raw emotion from her gaze. "This is probably going to sound pretty petty. But spending time with your family makes me feel even worse about mine. Yes, I have Olivia and I love her more than anything. But you have no idea how much I'd have given for what you have."

Her hands swung out as if painting the farmhouse and scenery around her. "This is perfect. This is ideal. You have a home, Trent. You have two parents who still love each other. You have three brothers, all of whom have dedicated their lives to taking care of others. The six of you are actually able to sit around a table and enjoy a meal together without bragging, competing, guilt-tripping or resentful silences. It's like something out of a fairy tale. Yet you spent your teen years rebelling like a brat and hanging out with people like Savannah?"

"I never dated Savannah!" His voice rose. "I know that probably doesn't seem important right now, but I need you to understand that. In her mind, we had a relationship. But my heart doesn't work like that. It doesn't connect with people. It can't. I can't explain it."

She stared at him. Wind tossed her hair around her face. "Try."

She really wanted to hear it? Fine.

"You think my family is perfect and ideal? Well, it's not. It's broken. And I'm the one who broke it. I'm really good at pretending to fit in. I'm good at talking to people, making superficial connections, getting people to like me and then moving on. But I don't do real relationships and I sure don't do vulnerability or romance.

It's like the part of me that knows how to give and receive love is broken."

At least, it had been until he'd met her. Something about being with Chloe had kicked the dust off his heart, pulled on its chain and tried to get it running again. Chloe had made his heart feel like it was capable of love. Until he'd gone and ruined everything with her, too.

"You've done and said a lot of foolish things since I've met you, Trent, but that lie you've somehow convinced yourself of is the worst!" Raw fire filled her gaze, burning a hole through his rusted chest. "Your heart isn't broken. You shut it off. You're like a kid who put himself in time-out, when nobody asked him to, and now has forgotten that all he has to do to get out of the corner is turn himself around. Don't forget, I was there when you passed out in the snow. I was there when your brothers brought you home. I was there when your mother and father saw them carry you in. I saw the looks on all their faces. More than that, I know you, Trent. And I know you have the biggest, strongest heart of anyone I've ever met—"

"Just a few hours ago, at Pit 11," he said, "you were shouting that I was so determined to shut people out, that I hurt everyone who cares about me and that I wreck everything I touch—"

"That was my cover talking!"

"Every good cover is based on a hint of truth!" He had to tell her. His mother was right to tell him to take her to the barn. He had to show her. It was the only way she'd understand. He stretched out his hand. "Come with me, please. There's something I need to show you."

She took his hand. They broke into a jog as he led her to the barn and they burst through the door, out of the snow. The warm, welcoming smell of hay filled his senses. They stood there in the darkness for a moment, panting, their eyes on each other as they waited for their vision to adjust to the lack of light. Then he slowly pulled his hand from hers, slid it onto her shoulder and turned her toward the side wall.

There, painted on the wood, was the outline of a girl, willowy and tall, carrying an old-fashioned torch in one hand and a schoolbag in another. A dark maze of lines spiraled down around her protectively like branches, joining more branches and flowers that grew up from the base.

Underneath read one word. *Faith*.

"Mom painted this," he said. "I used to have a sister. Her name was Faith. She was so unbelievably smart. She was always reading, and teachers loved her. We were in the same grade, even though she was over a year younger than me, because she was so quick at learning stuff, and I was so slow that school was like painful gibberish half the time.

"She'd make these supersmart jokes that I didn't understand. Then she'd laugh really, really loudly at them, even if nobody else was laughing. She had the loudest laugh of anyone I'd ever met and she never cared if she was the only one laughing.

"She died when she was twelve and I was thirteen. I was full of anger and full of pain. Uncle and the Wolfspiders took advantage of that. Because it was my... because I'd..."

He couldn't say the words. He couldn't tell the rest of the story. He'd never told it to anyone before and now the words wouldn't cross his lips. The old familiar sting of pain, anger and shame filled his core.

He turned away from Chloe and toward the wall that had born the brunt of his anger so many times as a teenager. His hand rose. His fingers balled into a fist. But he stayed his hand and wouldn't let the blow fly. He wasn't a young man anymore. He wasn't the person he'd been.

There was a dent in the wall in front of him, inches from where his fist would've landed. There was another dent, a few inches to the right and another a few inches to his left. He saw more dents, above him, below him, spreading out on all sides, and realized with a start that his father had never asked him to repair them or done it himself, but had left them there as a testament to the grief Trent had felt.

Emotion choked his throat, but not like the blind pain of the young man he'd been, more like the grief of a grown man who'd seen countless families torn apart by similar pain, violence and evil, and who knew he'd given every breath in his lungs to fight it.

His fingers unclenched. He braced his open palm against the wall.

"I've blamed myself for my sister's death," he said. "Because I wasn't there for her. She was murdered by a monster, because I let her down when she needed me the most."

* * *

Pain pierced Chloe's heart. Her hand slid over his back and up to his uninjured shoulder. He didn't flinch, but he also didn't turn. He stood there, his palm against the wall.

"I was supposed to meet up with her after school so we could walk home together," he said. "It was one of those rules that meant a lot to my parents, but from my perspective as an arrogant kid it seemed like nothing but a hassle. So I gave her the slip because I wanted to hang out with the cool kids behind the gym and bum a smoke without getting caught. I hid from Faith and made her walk home alone. Then I sauntered home an hour late, feeling cocky and like I'd pulled something off. Only, when I got here, Jacob was waiting outside for me, there were cop cars everywhere and my mom was… crying, howling, like I'd never heard anyone sob before.

"I didn't know that adults had been worried because some car had been seen cruising back roads, like a predator hunting for someone to hurt, or that two girls from another school had already been harassed by him but had gotten away. I never imagined that when Faith was walking home, alone, some predator would stop his car, grab her and try to…take…her…" Unshed tears choked the words from his throat.

"I'm so sorry," Chloe whispered.

She'd known so many girls and women like Faith. She'd dedicated her life to saving them, seeking justice for them and punishing those who'd hurt them. She'd hugged countless survivors and relatives as they'd grieved. She'd cried for them in the privacy of her own room and then come back, stronger, ready to fight another day. Now here she was, seeing the strongest and most amazing man she'd ever known being broken down by that same pain.

Lord, what a horrible weight and burden he's carried all these years. Help him to forgive himself. Help me to help him bear it. Help him to know he doesn't have to carry it alone.

She slipped into the space between his body and the wall and stood there, her back to the slats that had borne the brunt of his pain. Her arms slid around him. He bent down, until his forehead brushed hers. Her eyes closed. Tears slid down her face and onto his. They stood there, their foreheads touching and their chests beating into each other.

"The monster didn't succeed in abducting her," Trent whispered, his voice hoarse. "She fought back hard. She fought for her life and refused to let him take her. Police said she died quickly. That he choked her out in seconds and left her there. They said she died fighting."

"Sounds like she was very strong and very smart," Chloe said.

"Yeah, she was pretty tough." He chuckled, sadly. "Typical Henry."

His palm slid off the wall and around her waist. He held her there for a moment and she leaned up against the gentle rise and fall of his chest.

"They never found the guy," Trent added. "They found his skin under her fingernails and his blood on her hands. Police think it was because of her that he disappeared after that and left the area. His car was never seen again. They did DNA tests and compared him to everyone who could possibly be connected with her life. Nothing was a match. Jacob hasn't given up on finding the guy, though. That's part of what led him into Criminal Investigations."

"You realize that Jacob probably blames himself, too, as do your parents." She opened her eyes. Her hand brushed his jaw. "Look at me. You can't live your life punishing yourself for this. It's not what your smart, strong sister who loved to laugh would've wanted. You were just a kid. You had no way of knowing anything like that would happen. A predator like that was probably watching the area for weeks or months. If it hadn't been her, it would've been someone else or he might have targeted her another day in another place. You're a cop. You know this. We do our best, but sometimes we can't stop all evil from ever happening."

"I know." Blue eyes looked deeply into hers. "But in a way, knowing that makes it worse."

"I don't understand," she said. How was blaming himself better than accepting some things were out of his hands?

"Because as long as I keep blaming myself and telling myself that it was my fault, I can fool myself into thinking I had the power to stop it." His thumb brushed the trail of tears from her cheeks. "What's the worst option? Believing I failed? Or accepting that no matter how hard I fight and how hard I try, there are some villains I'm never going to catch and sometimes there's no way to prevent those I care about from getting hurt?

How do I let myself care about anyone knowing I'm incapable of protecting them?"

He closed his eyes again and she felt his breath on her lips. She closed her eyes, too, and Trent let out a long sigh that bordered on a groan. "How do I let myself love someone knowing I might lose them?"

"I don't know," Chloe whispered. "All I know is I can't control when I fall. I can only control where I land."

"Well, it feels like I'm falling," Trent said, "and all I know is that with you is where I want to land."

Trent's mouth brushed over hers, soft and deep. He kissed her in a way that felt like a request for forgiveness and a desire to be known. He kissed her like he'd meant it, and he always had, but had been too afraid to say so. She kissed him back, her hands in his hair and her body in his arms, like they were both falling and holding on to each other as they fell.

Her phone buzzed in her pocket. Then it buzzed a second time, a third and a fourth. She pulled away from the kiss. He stepped back and let her out of the embrace. She took out her phone. It kept buzzing. Message after message arriving. "Nick must've gotten the Wi-Fi working."

She had twenty-seven texts. From at least six different numbers.

Hey. I think I know who has payara. Hodge.

Hi, it's Aidan. Can we meet up and talk? I know who had the drugs. I didn't tell because he said they weren't his and I believe him. Also, have you seen Coach? They rescheduled the Haliburton game for tonight because of the fight and everything yesterday.

Hello, Detective. It's Brandon. If I talk to you, will you promise not to tell my grandfather?

'Sup. It's Johnny. Wanna talk? Want coffee?

Hi. It's Poppy. I think Johnny does steroids. I don't know about other drugs, though. Also, I'm really not dating him. He dates a lot of girls. He's kind of a player.

Hi. Can we talk? It's Lucy.

Hi, miss. I think I saw some pills in Brandon's bag one time and he tossed them in the garbage can. He said he thought someone had been messing in his bag. I didn't tell the police because I didn't know for sure and his grandfather is a jerk who'd stop paying his tuition and throw him in jail. Also I'm Milo.

"It's Third Line!" She laughed in a mixture of relief and amazement. Her thumb scrolled through the messages. Then she held up the phone and let him read. "I gave them this big speech last night after Royd was arrested about responsibility and stepping up. I told them it was up to them to stop the flow of payara and save their community. I told them all to text me whatever they knew about payara and they are!"

Trent stepped back and ran his hand over his jaw. "The third-line players are texting you about payara?"

"Yes." She watched as he read the messages. "See? They want to talk. They want to help. We have to question them again. If it's true that Brandon threw the drugs in the garbage can, that's a major breakthrough to finding out who's selling them. We have to go back to Bobcaygeon."

"No, we don't." Trent shook his head. "We have to follow the investigation and the investigation has moved so far beyond mere college students using pills at this point. It's not about Third Line anymore.

"It's about whoever Royd is working with and whatever he and the Wolfspiders are planning. We have other leads now. Like I told you, Coach Henri is gone. Eli has taken over the team and I sent in my resignation to Trillium."

"But the third-line players—" Chloe started.

"Were a means to an end," he interrupted softly. "You know that. I wasn't ever really their coach. I was there to get information out of them when we thought they were the best lead we had. Now we have better leads. This case isn't about four mediocre hockey players from a small-town community college anymore. Now we know the Gulos and the Wolfspiders are both somehow involved. The Wolfspiders ran us off the road last night. Not to mention, I'm injured. I'm not going back to Bobcaygeon."

"Well, I am." Chloe's chin rose. "You might be used to walking out of people's lives without saying goodbye and dropping your mask at the door. But I'm not, and that's not how I do my job. I made them a promise that if they were honest with me, I'd help them."

Cold wind rushed in through the door, sending it flying back on its hinges.

Trent was still shaking his head. He didn't get it. He probably never would. But she still had to try to explain.

"The story of my life is littered with people who just disappeared," she said. "People who promised to write letters I never heard from again. Friends who stopped talking to me because of some argument my father had with their father. Relationships that vanished overnight.

"We talked about broken parts of ourselves? Well, my father's shenanigans broke the part of me that knew how to trust. I asked these students to trust me. They are. I'm not letting them down. I'm going to listen to them. Maybe it won't help solve the payara case. But I can still put them in touch with lawyers, social workers, therapists, churches, support groups, Victim Services or whatever else they need. I'm going to show them that cops are worth trusting."

"I can't go back," he said again. His shoulders flinched and he winced, as if he'd tried to cross his arms before remembering his injured shoulder wouldn't let him. "For me, when a door is closed, it's closed. If you go back, I can't protect you."

"I never asked you to protect me." She slipped the phone in her pocket and grabbed his free hand in hers. "I don't need you to promise to keep me safe—even though I adore the fact that you want to try. What I need is someone who's there for me, day in and day out, who I can count on not to just disappear."

She watched as his eyes scanned the barn wall, as if drawing lines connecting all the holes he'd punched there.

"Let's walk," he said. "We need to talk. I told you this payara case was supposed to be just a short-term assignment tiding me over until a big gang investigation started. Well, it's pretty far away."

Her heart stopped. "How far?"

"Pretty far," he said. They stepped out of the shelter of the barn and back into the snow. "I'm going to be a long ways away and we won't be able to communicate while I'm gone."

Her eyes rose to the snow falling from above. Trent was disappearing from her life yet again. "How long will you be gone?"

"A really long time," he said. "I'm sorry. But I'll be going after a source we suspect is funding a lot of organized crime. It could be my opportunity to cripple the Wolfspiders, the Gulos and countless other gangs. It'll be a huge investigation."

"And you'll be the one on the inside," she said. "Why? There are dozens of excellent undercover officers. You could be leading them, guiding them, training them and overseeing their missions. You could be the running point from head office as part of a team, making the difference you want to make and still coming home at night, instead of walking away from everything you've got."

"What am I walking away from, Chloe? What specifically? Tell me. What's here that's worth staying for?" Something deep and aching echoed in his eyes and shook something inside her. There was a question there. One that he wasn't ready to speak and she didn't know how to answer. How could she tell him she loved him and ask him to stay, when he'd just end up leaving, anyway?

The sound of motors filled the air. Trent turned. A motorcade of beaten-up vehicles pulled into the driveway.

His face paled. "I'm so sorry, I was wrong! Run! Call the police. Tell my family to hide. Get them to safety." He pushed her shoulder. "Go!"

She turned and ran. Her footsteps pelted toward the farmhouse, even as questions swarmed her brain like the vehicles converging around the farmhouse. Then she saw the dented red truck that had run her off the road and the white van that had bumped them from behind. She saw the enforcers from the night before spilling from the vehicles and standing shoulder to shoulder like a shield.

Then she saw Uncle climbing out of a truck behind them.

"Trent!" Uncle called. "Glad to see you're still standing. Sorry for the unexpected house call, but I've got a brand-new problem, and you are going to be the solution. You have five minutes to tell your family and girlfriend goodbye, and then we're going for a drive." He turned to a large man holding a semiautomatic and gestured to Chloe. "Shoot her in the leg and then grab her. Trent's stubborn and will need to see what the penalty will be of him saying no."

THIRTEEN

Prayer filled Trent's heart as he watched the large, ugly gang enforcer set Chloe in his sights. What was Uncle doing here at his family's farm? How had he been so wrong? He'd believed all this time Uncle would keep to his word and leave his family alone.

"Stop!" Trent called. If he got in the vehicle with Uncle, he'd never make it out alive. But what other choice did he have? He couldn't let Chloe get hurt. He'd give up his own life, if that's what it took to save hers. "I'll go with you."

Uncle smirked, like a hunter that knew he'd finally found his prey's weakness. "Good. Tell your girlfriend to stop, drop to her knees and raise her hands."

"Chloe, stop!" Trent begged. "Trust me. It'll be okay."

But Chloe didn't stop. She ran, strong and straight, with her head down and elbows up, toward the enforcer like a linebacker. The enforcer fired. Chloe leaped. Bullets hit the snow beneath her. Her body struck the enforcer, knocking him back into the snow. He swore and leaped to his feet. But it was too late. Chloe had already scrambled up the front steps and through the front door as someone on the inside flung it open for her. The enforcer spun and shot at the space on the porch where she'd been just seconds before. The farmhouse's front window shattered.

"Uncle! You came for me! Here I am!" Trent shouted. His free hand rose. Could he take an armed Wolfspider enforcer down with a dislocated shoulder? Maybe. But there was no way he could take an entire army of them. Even if Chloe or Jacob was already on the phone with Dispatch it would take police at least fifteen minutes to get vehicles out to the farm. His best hope was to stall. "Are you really so scared of me that you had to bring everybody and his brother to talk to me? Come on! It's Christmas Eve. People have better things to do than stand around in the snow."

Ugly murmurs rippled through the crowd. The Wolfspiders knew as well as Trent did that if the man who never got his hands dirty was making a house call, it could only mean one thing: execution.

Lord, I knew from the first day I decided to walk back into the Wolfspiders' den as an undercover cop that my life could end like this. If I die today, let me die protecting those I love.

Uncle smirked. "What happened to your shoulder? Don't tell me you got into some kind of trouble after you left the grill last night."

"Fender bender with a reckless driver." Trent's smile grew tight. He prayed that the police were on the way and that his family had gotten to safety. Sure, Jacob was a decorated cop, Max had seen more than his fair share of trauma as a paramedic and Nick had served a term in the military. But they were grossly outmatched and this was his fight. "I thought you said you were going to let me and Royd sort things out between ourselves."

"I'm having a bit of a problem with Royd." Uncle's mouth curled into a scowl.

"Oh, really?" Trent blinked. "What kind of problem?"

"Our boy Royd called me this morning from jail and told me he'd found the payara dealer and the location of the lab." Uncle looked like even the memory of the conversation had left a bad taste in his mouth. "He claims he's made a deal with them to take over the operation. Thought it gave him leverage. Thought he could use it to negotiate with me for a new role in my organization."

Really? Wow. Well, Royd never had been the sharpest knife in the drawer and preferred brute force over thought and precision. But if Uncle thought that he could use Trent to teach Royd a lesson—let alone hurt whichever Third Line player was involved—he had another thought coming. He prayed it wasn't Brandon. Or Aidan. Or Milo. Or Hodge. It was funny. For months he'd been looking at the third-line players as suspects. Now he found himself hoping he'd been dead wrong. The thought of any of them being in trouble, like he'd once been, was unthinkable.

"Sounds like Royd betrayed you. I don't see what any of this has to do with me."

"Oh, you're going to fix this for me." Uncle's sneer grew into a vicious grin. "Obviously, I need to teach Royd a lesson. I reached out to the Gulos. Figured if they wanted payara so badly, it gave me a sweet opportunity to broker a deal. So we're going to team up, go after the supply chain together, find the lab, convince the manufacturer to work for us instead and then split the distribution."

Right, of course he was going to sell Royd out to a rival gang, leave it to them to track him down and kill him, once again keeping Uncle's own hands clean.

But what Uncle was describing was no less than a major shift in Canada's gang warfare power structure.

He couldn't imagine what leverage Uncle could have possibly used to make the Gulos agree to it, and the truce would be unlikely to last once Uncle had his hand on the payara supply. But until they did, it would be carnage. Finding and destroying the lab would be just the start, as they flushed out the next lab and the next, and took out anyone in their way. Who knew how many civilians and police would die and how much property would be destroyed in the process? What had happened at the sports center in Bobcaygeon was only the beginning.

Help me, Lord. Help me stop this.

Trent walked forward, knowing his voice was the only weapon he had left. "Again, what are you doing here? What does any of this have to do with me? I'm not about to help you kill Royd or broker a deal with the Gulos."

A chuckle spread through the crowd. It sent shivers up his spine and he didn't know why.

"Oh, yes, you are!" Uncle said. "You couldn't imagine how interested the Gulos were when I told them that the Wolfspiders had their very own undercover cop. One who'd also arrested countless Gulos and ruined several of their major operations. Not to mention someone who knew everything there was to know about drugs, weapons and human trafficking in Canada, including the location of secret dens, trade routes, where the various people have hidden their money and the identity of other undercover cops. A treat as sweet as a dirty cop like you was just too good for one gang to keep all to themselves. Just imagine what they'd do to a cop like that and the information they'd pull from him once I turned him over."

So, Uncle hadn't just negotiated a truce with the Gulos to punish Royd and take over the payara operation. He'd offered up Trent as bait. No wonder they hadn't come back sooner to finish the job after the crash. He was confident Uncle wasn't foolish enough to give up Trent's actual identity without a deal being made, so he was going to deliver Trent to the Gulos himself. Trent grit his teeth as his eyes rose to the sky in prayer.

Lord, I can't let them take me. I can't let the Gulos force me to tell them all I've learned during my career. Too many lives hang in the balance. But if I don't, what happens to my family and Chloe?

"My promise not to harm your family as long as you obey me still stands," Uncle said, as if reading his mind. "I won't touch them, even after you're dead. Everybody knows I'm a man of my word. But, you try anything, and we'll swarm your parents' house and burn it to the ground. Now, hands on your head. You're coming with us."

The door creaked behind him.

"He's not going anywhere." Chloe's voice filled the air.

Chloe, please, go back inside. Can't you see how outnumbered we are? You can't give up your life for me.

He turned. Chloe stood on the front porch of his family home, her service weapon held strong and firm in one hand and her badge in the other. But she wasn't alone. Jacob stood beside her in full uniform, holding his service weapon. Nick stood beside him in his fatigues, armed with the gun he'd gotten for his nineteenth birthday, and Max stood beside him, his paramedic's bag at his feet and Dad's new hunting rifle at his shoulder. Then Trent saw his father holding his older hunting revolver and this mom with the family's shotgun in one hand and the phone to her ear. His whole family— everyone he loved—stood on the front porch of the farmhouse, weapons at the ready, willing to defend his life.

"Go back inside!" Trent yelled. "Now! Go inside and lock the door! This is going to get ugly and none of you are going to die for me!"

"We're Henrys, son." Tears filled his father's eyes. "Henrys never go down without a fight."

"Don't you get it? I need to protect you!" *Like I didn't protect Faith.*

"No, you don't!" Jacob cut him off firmly. "Don't you get it, Trent? We already lost one of us. We're not losing another."

He did. Suddenly and overwhelmingly, as he looked from face to face and saw that same fierce, protective love he felt for each one of them filling their eyes for him in return. He could see the forgiveness he'd never let himself see. He could feel the wall he'd built around his heart crumbling in rubble at his feet.

"Enough!" Uncle snapped. He pushed past the Wolfspiders protecting him. "You're outnumbered. Trent, I own you. I will always own you and I will kill you when I'm ready. And if any of them try to get in my way, I will kill them, starting with your detective fiancée."

The single gunshot rang loud and clear, striking Uncle in the shoulder, and Trent watched as the man who'd threatened his life ever since he was a teenager crumpled to his knees in the snow.

The Wolfspiders hesitated. The large enforcer raised his weapon and aimed it toward the house. Trent leaped on him from behind, knocking him to the ground one-handed. The sound of police and emergency vehicles filled the air. A pair of handcuffs appeared at the corner of Trent's vision. He looked up, expecting Chloe. It was Jacob. Trent let his brother take over the arrest and cuff the enforcer. Then he pulled himself to his feet.

A mass of shouts and motors filled the air. Wolfspiders rushed to their vehicles even as police poured down the driveway, cornering them. Then he saw Max down on his knees beside Uncle, tending to his wound. Chloe was at Uncle's other side, arresting him.

"Chloe shot the bullet that took down Uncle," Jacob said. "It's a nonfatal through-and-through. She said something about how you'd told her not to shoot him until he actually explicitly threatened to kill either one of you. Her nerves are amazing."

"She's incredible." Trent stood there for a moment and watched as Chloe read Uncle his rights. Then he stepped back and waited while Jacob handed the enforcer off to another officer. The sheer volume of vehicles swarming the farmhouse lawn was unbelievable. There were dozens of officers in full riot gear, taking down criminal after criminal. It was like something out of a dream. He watched as Chloe went over and introduced herself to the officer in charge. Jacob came back to Trent. "How on earth did you make this happen?"

"Don't look at me," Jacob said. "Chloe made all the calls. I was busy giving the rest of the family a crash course on the Criminal Code of Canada sections on reasonable force in terms of self-defense and protections of others. Dad wasn't about to let some Wolfspiders storm the old farmhouse or kidnap you."

"You didn't think try to convince our family not to get into a standoff with criminals?" Trent asked.

"What can I say? We're all Henrys." Jacob chuckled. "But in all seriousness, Chloe mobilized this operation. People came out of the woodwork in an instant to make this happen, like nothing I've ever seen before. Your fiancée's reputation is stellar."

He could tell his big brother was trying to make a joke. But it wasn't funny.

"You know that Chloe and I aren't actually in a romantic relationship," Trent said.

"Whose fault is that?" Jacob said. "You do realize

you're just standing here, while she's over there making what should be the biggest arrest of your career?"

"I know." He guessed that under any other circumstances watching another cop take down the man he'd waited years to arrest would sting somewhat. But somehow this was better. "It's okay. It's good for her to have Uncle's arrest on her record. You know she's in the running for the next detective sergeant post that opens up? She'll get it, too. Only like twelve percent of all senior officers are women. She'll be one of them."

Jacob's eyes searched his brother's face. "And what do you want?"

"I want to marry her," Trent admitted. "Not that I'd ever ask. And not that I expect she'd ever say yes. I've never even really admitted to her that I have feelings for her. It's all push and pull with us. One step forward, two steps back.

"We had a moment in the barn where I told her about Faith and it was like something changed between us. But when I told her that I was heading off on another undercover mission, the roller coaster crashed right back down again. She needs someone steady. I'm not steady. I assume a different cover identity every few weeks." Or at least, that's what he'd always told himself.

Jacob didn't answer. Instead the two cops just stood there for a long moment and watched the police operation unfold around them. Then Trent ran his hand over his head. "I need to think and I need to pray. Can you cover for me if I take a walk? I won't leave the farm. I just think that Chloe and I need to have a long talk, and I want to get my head on straight first."

"Sure thing." Jacob clasped Trent's good shoulder in a quick half hug.

Trent turned and walked up the hill to the tree line of the Henry farm. He brushed the snow off a log and sat gazing down on the scene below.

Lord, I don't even know what to pray for right now. To ask You for a happily-ever-after with Chloe feels selfish. But, if You help me find a way, I'll love and protect her with all the strength You've given me.

The wind whistled in the trees. The number of lights circling below slowly diminished as vehicle after vehicle pulled out of the driveway. Finally he saw a solitary figure, tall and strong in dark green fatigues, climbing up the hill toward him. He stood. "Nick, hey!"

"Chloe took off," Nick said. "One of the other officers lent her their personal car to drive to Bobcaygeon."

"What?" Trent leaped to his feet. Chloe was gone? Just like that? "Did you guys tell her where I was?"

"Of course we did." His little brother shrugged and ran one hand through his chestnut hair. Nick wasn't much older than the third-line players. "But she's as stubborn as you and didn't want to be convinced. Not that we didn't try. I don't pretend to get it. I'm the wrong person to ask about what women mean when they say things. Mom or maybe Jacob could explain it better than me. I got the impression Chloe thought you'd done a disappearing act on her and she said she was in a hurry to get to a hockey game."

The youngest of the Henry boys could understand anything mechanical or practical. But relationships weren't his strong suit.

Trent groaned. "I'm guessing you all had a quick family meeting and you drew the short straw to come be the one to tell me that Chloe'd left me?"

"Nah, bro." A grin filled Nick's face. He reached into his pocket and pulled out a pair of car keys. "I pulled the long straw! I'm the one who gets to drive when you go chasing after her."

Chloe locked the doors of the borrowed car and walked through the parking lot toward the Bobcaygeon Sports Center. It had been a long, silent drive through the snow. She'd kicked herself the whole way.

Driving away from Trent had been painful, agonizing even, and his family's attempts to delay her hadn't helped. What would the point have been? Trent had taken off, and she wasn't about to go chasing after him, just so they could have yet another argument hashing out what she already knew. Trent was leaving, no matter what she said or did.

And she loved him, no matter how hard she'd tried to stop her foolish heart from falling. She loved him for all his strengths, all his faults and everything about him that drove her crazy.

Something inside her had started falling for him that very first moment she'd seen those fierce, brave and compassionate blue eyes shining through the rough exterior of his Wolfspider cover. It had only continued to grow through every new and complicated version of Trent she met, like each cover he'd worn had revealed a new truth about the heart of the man who lay inside. But she also knew that her own heart was going to keep breaking over him, unless she was the one who finally gave up and walked away. She'd hung on for far too long to a dream that wasn't ever going to come true.

She stepped into the front entrance and joined the throng of people pressing toward the hockey rink. Her phone rang. She glanced down. It was a blocked number. Hope leaped in her chest. She stepped into an empty hallway and raised the phone to her ear. "Hello? Trent?"

"Hi? Detective Brant?" The voice was young, female and frightened. "Is that you?"

"It is." Chloe's voice dropped. She walked deeper into the empty hall. "Who's this?"

"Lucy... Brandon's sister..."

"Hi, Lucy, of course I remember you..." Chloe walked farther down the hall. The sounds of the crowd faded. "What's up?"

"I made the payara."

"You did what?" Chloe's footsteps froze. Lucy had been making the payara? The young woman behind the coffee counter that she'd saved from the Gulos? Staff Sergeant Butler's timid, nineteen-year-old granddaughter? "I needed money to move to Vancouver to go take cosmetics chemistry, and someone told me there was big money in inventing new pills. He told me he'd pay me really well if I did. So, I made payara."

"Who was that someone?" Chloe could feel her heart beating like a warning drum against her rib cage. Lucy didn't answer. "You're Trilly, aren't you? What happened last night?"

"The guy I told you about found my phone and made me text you. I didn't know that other guy was going to attack you. I promise I didn't! Now he's says he's made some business deal, and we've got to pack up right away and go somewhere. And I don't want to go."

"Who? Who's making you do this, Lucy?" Her brother, Brandon? Her grandfather, Staff Sergeant Butler?

"I can't tell you!"

"Yes, you can!" Frustration and compassion merged in Chloe's heart. The complex relationship between abusers and victims was one of the hardest and most agonizing parts of her job. She'd lost count of how many young women who'd begged to be rescued then went back to their dealer or abuser before the trial. She prayed to God for patience and wisdom. "Where are you now?"

"In the sports center." There was a pause and then a sniffle. "I'm in the basement in the storage room where we keep things for the coffee stand. I was making payara there."

Chloe looked down at the tiles. The payara lab was in the sports center. It had been underneath them the whole time. Her footsteps quickened. "Stay right there. I'm coming to you. Just hang on, okay!" She found a utility door and pushed through into the stairwell. Her feet pounded down the stairs into the basement. The door swung shut behind her. "I'll be there in a moment—"

"Detective!" A voice boomed behind her as she watched the rectangular light cast by the open door grow wider. She turned. Johnny was standing at the top of the stairs, holding the door open. "I was hoping I'd see you! Where are you going? Thought we could grab a coffee or something."

"Johnny, hi!" Was he kidding her with this? A young,

male lothario was exactly the kind of distraction she didn't need right now.

She turned back to the phone. "Don't go anywhere, please. I'll be there in a minute." But the line had already gone dead.

"What are you doing hanging out down here?" Johnny lumbered down the stairs toward her. Light dimmed as the door swung shut again. "I was keeping an eye out. Then I saw you and waved. But I guess you didn't see me." He stopped one step above her. "So is it true you and Coach split up? I heard he just quit and took off."

"It's complicated," she said, and nothing she planned to discuss now. "Please, just head back upstairs to the game."

He stepped closer, his head tilted to the side. "But what are you doing down here? You sure you don't need somebody to keep you safe?"

"I'm meeting someone. It's police business. You understand."

"Yeah, I understand." He pressed a gun into her side. "And I'm sorry. Because I really don't want to hurt you."

FOURTEEN

Nick pulled his truck to a stop in the sports center parking lot and turned to Trent. "Do you want me to come in with you? Because I should really go get gas and maybe a bite to eat."

"Nah, thanks, I'm good." Trent leaped out the passenger door. "Just don't forget to come back. I might not find Chloe and even if I do, she might not feel like driving me all the way home. I still have no clue what I'm going to say to her."

His little brother chuckled and leaned over the front seat. "I'll tell you a secret, but you gotta promise not to tell the folks. I had a girlfriend on base. Not too proud of how it all went down. Never told Mom and Dad, because I knew they wouldn't approve. It ended badly, and she was so mad I thought for a moment she was going to stab me with a pair of scissors."

Trent's eyebrow rose. "The moral of the story is don't let Chloe near scissors?"

"No, it was just something she said to me. She told me she'd didn't care what my words were, she'd just always hoped I would fight harder for her." He grinned, but his gaze ran to the sky above. "Maybe I should've. But, anyway, my point is that you should go fight for Chloe. Maybe it's not about knowing what to say. It's about just showing up."

"Thanks. I'll give you a call in a few, hopefully with good news." Trent slammed the door with his good hand and walked through the parking lot. *Lord, I wasn't joking. I don't know what to say to her. I don't know what to do. I just know that I love her. I don't know if that's enough.*

His phone began to ring. His heart leaped. It was her. He answered. "Hi! Chloe, I'm here—"

But instantly his voice faded as he heard the steady tap of her fingers drumming SOS in Morse code against the microphone.

"Johnny, put the gun down!" Chloe's voice was muffled. "I'm just putting my phone in my pocket, like you told me to."

Johnny? The Haliburton team center?

His footsteps quickened across the parking lot. Nick's truck was already disappearing down the road. Chloe was in danger and had called him for help. But where was she? He closed his eyes and listened. An ache filled his heart. She had no idea he was even there. She'd called him to give him information about the case. Maybe she'd even called him to say goodbye. Then he heard the sound of footsteps echoing down an empty hallway.

"Johnny, what is this?" Chloe asked. "Why do you

have a gun? How did you even convince Lucy to create a payara lab in the basement of the sports center?"

"You've got this all twisted," Johnny said. "I'm not a bad guy. I threw a rock through the window at you when I found out Lucy had called you, because I thought that might convince you to leave it alone. Now everything's a great big mess and I've got some major problems. I'll get you out of here. We just need to get Lucy first."

"Put the gun down and we'll talk. You don't want to hurt me. You're not a killer. You told me in the gym that you're a tech genius and an entrepreneur."

"I am!" Johnny's voice grew defiant. "I just did business with the wrong people and got in some trouble. But I'm going to fix it. And it'll be fine."

"What kind of wrong people? You mean a gang? You mean the Gulos or the Wolfspiders? I can help you. But not until you put the gun down."

Trent paused outside, beneath the lights of the Christmas tree. People were still streaming through the front door. He wanted to be in the building. But once he joined the crowd he'd lose his ability to hear her. *Keep him talking. I'm here. I'm listening. Tell me what I need to know. Tell me how to rescue you.*

"So, this is your grand plan?" Chloe asked. "Forcing Lucy to make drugs for you? Becoming a common drug dealer?"

"I'm not a common drug dealer!" Johnny's voice rose. "I came up with the idea of inventing a new designer drug. I talked Lucy into it. I found sellers. I got Nicole's passwords to get access to the police computer systems and police scanner, so I always knew what they knew—"

"Constable Docker was helping you? Why?"

Johnny snickered. "She thought we were dating."

"Lucy thinks you're dating, too, doesn't she?"

"Maybe," Johnny said. "And don't believe Poppy. That picture is totally her. But it was a one-off just to get Hodge to fly off the handle, to create a diversion."

He laughed again and Trent's blood boiled. He looked up to the snow falling from the dark purple sky. Was that how he'd come across? Using people and not realizing who he'd hurt? *Forgive me, Lord.* If so, it had never been on purpose. But it would never happen again. He'd get down on his knees and ask Chloe to make an honest man of him. Just as soon as he found her.

"You found out Lucy had contacted me," Chloe said. Was it his imagination or had their footsteps slowed? "So you tossed me to Royd to take care of. I'm guessing you also overheard that Gulo bellowing that I had his phone, and tipped Royd off about that, too."

Trent nodded as he listened. It was all making sense now. He just wished he'd realized this sooner, before Chloe's life was on the line.

"Royd's crazy." Johnny's voice darkened. "I thought I could play him, but he's a psycho. He told me he's going to make the Gulo attack on the sports center look like child's play. He said he wired bombs to the fire alarm system, so if anyone pulls a fire alarm it sets off the timer to go into countdown mode, giving him just enough time to run out of the building. If you call the police, he'll know. He has my police scanner. He gave us twenty minutes to get all our lab stuff out of the building and leave with him, or he'll set the bomb and *ka-boom*."

Trent's footsteps hurried toward the sports center. A scenario unfolded in his mind. So, Chloe was being held captive by Johnny and presumably they were going to wherever Lucy was. That meant only one hostile who was in over his head. That also gave him twenty minutes to evacuate the building, disarm Johnny, rescue Chloe and Lucy, and call the police. Not easy, but doable. The sound of footsteps slowed. Wherever in the building they were, they'd arrived.

"What is this?" Royd's voice boomed down the phone line. "What is she doing here?"

Royd was already out of jail? Had someone inside the police messed up his arrest or not charged him correctly? Or did Royd have a connection on the inside? Anything was possible. Any faith Trent had in Butler's division had been steadily disappearing ever since this whole mess had started. True, it had been over twenty-four hours since Royd's arrest, so likely he was just out on bail. Trent knew the police might not hold him for long if they'd booked him for assault and not attempted kidnapping. Still, he had hoped that Butler's division would have tried to find a way to hold him longer.

Trent's footsteps quickened.

"I thought we could use her or something," Johnny said.

"You thought wrong," Royd snapped.

Then he heard the sound of a struggle, the phone fell and a gunshot echoed on the line. Chloe cried out. The phone went dead. Trent's heart leaped into his throat. *Oh, Lord, what do I do?* He could save an arena full of people. He could try to save Chloe and Lucy. He couldn't do both. He needed backup. He needed help. He grabbed his phone and dialed.

"Hey, Coach," Brandon answered. "Look, I really don't know what you want but none of the guys want to talk to you right now."

"Listen to me, I need Third Line. Right now. All of you. Meet me in the alley behind the sports center."

"We're already getting changed and I really don't know if I can convince the guys. Everyone's still pretty angry at you."

"I know," Trent said. "I don't blame you and I can explain. But Chloe and Lucy are in danger. Please."

"I'll see what I can do."

Trent ran for the alley. It was empty. He paced while he prayed.

The door creaked.

"Hey, Coach." Aidan's voice came from behind him. "You got some nerve disappearing like that. What happened to your beard?"

He turned, hope filling his heart as Aidan, Brandon, Milo and Hodge filed out into the alley, in various stages of street clothes and hockey gear. Four pairs of skeptical eyes focused on his face. Arms crossed. Mouths frowned. He took a deep breath and pulled out his badge.

"My name is Detective Trent Henry. I'm a detective with the RCMP. I've been undercover as your coach for the past three months, because police thought one of the four of you was selling payara."

Various stages of anger and denial filled their faces. He was surprised none of them swore at him.

"You what?" Hodge found his voice first. "What is this?"

"I get that you're angry," Trent said. "Believe me when I say I understand. You're all great people and I was wrong to think any of you was behind payara. But Johnny talked Lucy into making it. He has her and Chloe trapped somewhere in the building with a criminal named Royd, who wired a bomb to the fire alarm and is threatening to blow the whole place up."

"I don't believe you!" Aidan snorted. "You're trying to tell me that Brandon's little sister is involved in a drug scheme?"

But one look at Brandon's pale face and Trent could tell that he believed it.

"You're the one who left the payara in the locker room, weren't you, Brandon?" Trent said. "You found it in your bag and didn't know how it had gotten there, so you just hid it a garbage can where it was found by the janitor and turned over to police. The rest of Third Line covered for you. Right?"

Brandon looked down but didn't argue.

Trent took that as a yes. "Well, if your sister didn't put it there, who did? My guess is that she used your bag to get drugs to Johnny during a game, or one of you two grabbed the wrong bag somehow, but either way you had no idea what they were doing there, so your friends agreed to cover for you."

"This is nonsense and I'm not going to stand around listening to it!" Aidan turned to leave. "None of us had anything to do with making or selling payara. So what if Brandon found pills in his bag one time and we all covered for him? We all knew they couldn't be his. You've been lying to our faces for months. Why should we believe anything you say now?"

"My little sister was murdered when I was thirteen and I blamed myself," Trent said. "Trust me, even if this isn't your fault, you don't want this on your conscience.

"You're right. I haven't been straight with you. But Chloe has. She came back here to help you. Now she and Lucy are in trouble. Everyone in this building is in danger. I'm taking a huge risk in blowing my cover to you guys, because if you tell people who I am, or post anything about this online, my days of working undercover taking down gang operations are over. But I need your help. I can't do this alone."

Silence fell. The guys were looking from one to the other. This was hopeless. They had no reason to trust him.

"Tell me one thing you've said to us since the day we met that wasn't a lie," Hodge said.

"I really do want to marry Chloe. She's not really my fiancée or anything. That part was a cover. But my feelings for her are totally real, and I'd like her to be my wife."

There was another pause that lasted a lot longer than he liked. He could almost feel the moments ticking by.

Then Brandon nodded. "Okay, I'm in. What do you need?"

"I need you to help me find Chloe and Lucy, and someone to evacuate the building without pulling the fire alarm so it doesn't set off the bomb."

"I'll disable the fire alarm," Milo said. "Then if anybody pulls it, nothing will explode."

"I can help you to find Lucy," Brandon said. "I know roughly where in the building she hangs out. But I didn't know what she was doing."

Trent let out a long sigh. "Okay, that leaves Aidan and Hodge to evacuate the building. Everyone good?"

They nodded. Then Aidan stuck his hand out in the middle of the circle and Third Line piled their hands in. Trent placed his hand on top and whispered a prayer. Then they ran.

Pain shot through Chloe's right leg, from where Royd's bullet had grazed it. Her arms ached from the zip tie fastening her hands together behind her back. She was down on the damp, concrete floor of a storage room, watching helplessly as Johnny and Lucy packed equipment into crates and Royd supervised, gun in hand.

Please, Lord, whatever happens to me, may my phone call to Trent have given him enough information to make sure justice is done.

"Lucy, Johnny, you don't have to go with him," she said. "You have a choice."

"Shut up, you!" Royd turned and focused his gun on Chloe.

Johnny's face had gone pale. Royd had taken his gun. "It'll be fine," he said. "Royd knows people. He'll set us up somewhere where Lucy can have a lab and he'll help my business expand. We'll be fine."

"You'll be owned by a gang member!" Chloe's voice rose. "What do you think life in a gang is like, Johnny? Because it's not all fancy parties and flashy cars. It's violence, ugliness and constantly looking over your shoulder wondering who you've got to be afraid of hurting or killing you."

"I said, stop talking!" Royd cuffed her across the face. Pain exploded through her jaw. He glanced at the clock. "Hurry up. I'm not waiting all night."

Lucy's hands shook so hard the glass beakers rattled.

"Listen to me, Lucy, Johnny's just using you." Chloe grit her teeth and talked through the pain. "Just like he used Poppy and Nicole. He doesn't love you. He's never going to protect you from people like Royd."

Lucy didn't look at her. She was on her last box now. The fire alarm switch loomed bright and red on the wall, like a giant self-destruct button.

"That's it," Royd growled. The gun jabbed hard into Chloe's forehead. "I thought maybe I could use you for some kind of leverage. But you're just too much trouble."

Her eyes closed. Silent prayers fell from her lips.

"Royd, put the gun down. This isn't going to end well for you." The voice was deep and strong, and it filled her heart with hope. She opened her eyes.

Trent was standing in the doorway, with Brandon behind him. Trent's eyes met hers. His voice dropped. "Hey, Chloe."

"Trent, you're here."

"Well, seemed only fair to return the favor," he said. But his eyes were serious as they looked at the gun digging into her flesh. Then he turned to the criminal behind it. "Royd, you and I go way back. So, I'll make you a deal. If you let Chloe, Lucy, Brandon and Johnny leave, I'll let you take me as a hostage in their place."

"On your knees, both of you." Royd's eyes cut toward the doorway. "You're in no position to bargain and nobody's going anywhere. You so much as move and I'm going to put a bullet right through her head. Got that?"

"Got it." Trent knelt. His eyes closed and she watched as a silent prayer moved across Trent's lips. Then his eyes met hers. Worry filled his gaze. She had a bullet wound in one leg, her hands tied behind her back and a gun aimed at her forehead, while Trent still had his shoulder in a sling and was down on his knees. But somehow, through all that, she felt safer than she had in a long time.

"Johnny," Royd snapped. "Handcuff them."

The athlete grabbed a zip tie then hesitated, looking at the shoulder sling. He handcuffed Trent to the metal shelf by the door. Then he glanced from Trent to Brandon and back again, and reached for a new zip tie. "I'm sorry about this. But I kind of have to."

"Guess dabbling in crime isn't turning out to be as much fun as you hoped," Trent said. He glanced sideways at Johnny, like Royd wasn't even there. This was one of his favorite tactics—verbal warfare, using his words as a weapon to get under a criminal's skin. "I've been there. Believe it or not, Royd here got me messed up and involved in crime when you all were still babies. Don't worry. I'm going to cause a distraction in a minute. When that happens, Brandon I want you to grab Lucy by the hand and run. Johnny, I sure hope you wise up and run, too. Trust me, you don't want to work for Royd."

Johnny paused inches away from Brandon. The zip tie shook in his hands.

"Are you trying to anger me, talking like that, Trent?" Royd snapped. "I don't know what game you think you're playing. But if you try anything, I'm going to shoot Chloe." He glanced at Johnny and Lucy. "Now, see how big a mess you two caused by involving a detective in this?"

"Now!" Trent shouted.

Royd glanced toward him to stop whatever he thought he was about to pull. Chloe dove forward, head-butting Royd in the chest. The gun fired into the ceiling. Lucy ran toward her brother. Brandon grabbed her by the arm. Their footsteps echoed down the hall. Johnny paused. His eyes darted around the small, collapsing empire he'd created. Then he turned and bolted after them.

Royd scrambled to his feet. The barrel of the gun swung from Chloe to Trent and back again. "Nice trick. You think this is funny? Neither of you are making it out of here alive. I'll set the timer and go after them, leaving the two of you to blow up in this building."

He yanked the fire alarm. Nothing happened. He swore.

Trent glanced at Chloe. "Milo really is an excellent electrician."

"I've had enough of you, Trent." Royd swung around and pointed the gun at him. "All my life you've acted like you're somehow better than me. When you quit the Wolfspiders and joined the police, I thought you were gone from my life for good. But you came back, and you kept coming back, again and again, convincing everyone you were special. Well, now I'm the one with the power. I'm the one that's going to run payara distribution in Canada. You've got one arm in sling and the other tied to a shelf. Your girlfriend has been shot in the leg and has her hands tied behind her back. I've got the only gun in the room. And I'm going to destroy the only thing you've ever cared about right in front of your eyes."

A fierce and determined grin curved Trent's lips.

That dangerous spark she loved so much flickered in his eyes as Chloe pulled herself up onto her knees. Her eyes met Trent's. He held her gaze.

Royd turned and aimed the barrel of the gun between Chloe's eyes.

Trent roared in pain as he yanked the shelf from its bolts so hard the handcuff snapped free.

Royd fired.

Chloe dropped to the floor and rolled.

Trent threw himself on Royd and wrestled the gun from his hand with one hand. Then he rolled Royd onto his stomach and pinned him to the ground with his knees and one good hand.

"What happened to those zip ties Johnny was holding?" Trent grunted.

Royd was still struggling and swearing.

Chloe tuned him out like white noise. "By the door," she said. "But what do you expect me to do with them, Cop Boy? My hands are still tied behind my back."

"Okay, fine," Trent said. "Turn your back to me. I'll pin him with my legs and cut your hands free."

"Got it!" She spun her back to him and waited as he yanked a knife from his pocket. The blade slipped between her wrists. He cut her hands free. She lunged for the zip ties and, with Trent's help, forced Royd's wrists together and cuffed them. "What's his full name again?"

"Roy Denver. Teachers would call out 'Roy D' in class, so he insisted we call him Royd, even before he started using steroids."

"Got it." Chloe pulled out her badge and stuck it in front of his face. "Let's try this again. Roy Denver. I am arresting you…"

Her eyes met Trent's. The affection and respect echoed there filled her heart with joy. But still there was a question hovering in their blue depths that gave her pause.

Now what? Now that the case was over and the source of the payara had been found, what happened now?

FIFTEEN

Snow fell in thick white flakes, swirling down from the dark sky above. People huddled in clumps behind the safety tape as police swept the sports center for both the remains of the drug lab and the hidden explosives. Flashing lights from emergency vehicles spun white and red, casting the scene in an odd, ethereal glow.

The staff of Nanny's Diner was serving hot chocolate and cookies. A group of the sports fans and players had gathered around the Christmas tree, phones raised above them like pinpoints of light as they sang Christmas carols. Christmas was only a couple of hours away and in the midst of the chaos the community had gathered together.

Trent paced in front of the yellow police tape like a tiger prowling his cage, his eyes scanning the emergency vehicles and staff for one face—Chloe.

After calling 9-1-1, he'd dragged Royd's squirming and defiant form out of the sports center while Chloe hopped alongside him, using a broom handle as a crutch. Thankfully the gun wound had been not much more than a surface scrape and the police had arrived quickly.

"Go," Chloe had told him. "None of these cops know you as anything more than a hockey coach. You might as well try to preserve as much of your cover as you can."

He'd tried to argue that now that Third Line knew the truth of his cover, it was probably spreading like wildfire through the student body, until it ended up online, killing any opportunity of future undercover work. But Chloe had been insistent. So he'd waited until the paramedics reached her then he'd slipped back into the crowd and found his brother Nick and filled him in. That had been almost an hour ago. Nick had wandered off into the crowd, either because he realized his older brother needed space or because Trent's restlessness was driving him nuts.

It was Chloe's case now. She got the glory. He prayed it would lead her to the promotion she'd earned and deserved more than any cop he'd ever known. And when she was done and came looking for him, she would find him there, waiting for her.

Lord, what will I say to her? Where do I start?

"Um, Coach?" Aidan's voice came from behind him. He turned. All four members of Third Line stood in the darkness.

"Guys! You were incredible!" His head shook, as he looked from face to face. "I'm in awe. Seriously. You disabled the alarm. You evacuated the arena." He glanced at Brandon. "You saved your sister's life. I'm so sorry I didn't have faith in you all before. I've never met a more impressive group of young men."

Feet shuffled. Eyes glanced at the ground, at the sky and at everywhere but him.

"It was nothing," Hodge said.

Right, he knew that tune. He'd played it many times himself. "How's Lucy?"

"Good." Brandon nodded. "She's shaken and scared. I'm not excusing what she did, but when she got in over her head with Johnny she was too scared of my grandfather to get help. Chloe introduced her to someone from Victim Services and also a detective friend of hers, and promised she'd be taken care of."

Trent let out a sigh of relief and nodded. "That's good."

"Johnny tried to run," Aidan said. A slight smirk turned his lips. "But Hodge and I saw him running. We caught up with him and made sure he stayed put. But just until the cops could arrest him, of course."

Trent chuckled. His eyes instinctively turned back to the flashing emergency lights. Chloe wouldn't leave without saying goodbye again, would she?

"Coach?" Brandon's voice dragged his attention back to the group. "One more thing. We all talked and decided, collectively as a group, that none of us are going to ever talk about anything you told us about yourself in the alley. Not a word.

"We told the police the truth—that you were our hockey coach and that you'd told us Chloe and Lucy were in trouble. But they didn't ask us if we knew anything else about you and we didn't volunteer that we did. We just wanted you to know that. You can trust us. We have your back. You are Coach Henri to us, and always will be. End of story. We promise."

Trent swallowed hard and let out a long breath. They were protecting his cover. He'd put his life in their hands and given them the opportunity to both blow his cover and ruin his career. Instead they'd promised to protect his cover and guard his secret. "Thank you. I really appreciate that."

"No problem," Aidan said. "We owe you that much."

Trent stuck his hand in the middle of the circle and they piled their hands on top, like a team huddle or sealing a pack. "If you ever need me, for anything, you call me, okay? I'll keep this phone number forever."

There were more nods and a couple of claps on his good shoulder. Then they glanced at something behind him and, as if with one mind, disappeared into the crowd. He looked back. Chloe was making her way toward him on crutches. Her eyes met his.

She smiled. He leaped the police tape and ran toward her. But before he could reach her, she raised one crutch and waved him off. "Don't you dare try to pick me up or I'll throttle you."

His hands rose. "But you're wounded."

"I'm fine. I'm just limping a bit."

"Got it." A grin turned the corner of his lips. "Well, there's a bench over there by the tree. Can I at least convince you to limp over there with me?"

She pretended to frown but the smile in her eyes gave her away. "Sure."

They walked slowly through the snow together, side

by side, toward the sparkling swell of lights around the Christmas tree. He lifted the police tape to let her pass underneath, feeling something swell in his chest as her head brushed against his arm.

"I was just talking to Brandon," he said. "He said that Lucy is willing to cooperate fully and you found her help?"

"She's still a bit uncertain, and I understand," Chloe said. "Trust can be hard. Johnny's been arrested. I don't know what hope there is for him, but people do change and he's young.

"Butler is definitely going to be facing an internal investigation now. Nicole Docker probably will, too. It's her fault Royd got bail after just one night in jail. She knew he was a friend of Johnny's, so just booked him on a basic assault charge. But with everything we have against Royd now, he'll be looking at being behind bars for a very long time." She waited while he brushed the snow off the bench. They sat. "How's Third Line?"

"They seem determined to protect my cover," he said. "They're pretty amazing people."

"They are," she said softly. "So, I guess this means there's nothing to stop you from taking that big and long case somewhere far, far away."

"It was in the Arctic, actually," he said.

Her green eyes looked deep into his. "That's pretty far."

"It is." He took her gloved hand in his and held it. His fingers stroked hers. "And I've decided I'm not going."

Her eyes grew wider. Something flickered in their depths. It was beautiful and something he'd rarely seen there. Hope. He knew in an instant he'd move heaven and earth to see it there every day. He took off his gloves. "You made a good point about letting someone else go undercover for once and my becoming part of the planning, training and coordinating team. I've got a lot of experience and there are a lot of young cops who could benefit. My shoulder's wonky. Plus, it would be nice to have a job that enabled me to still come home at night."

"I understand the feeling," she said. "If I get this promotion to detective sergeant, then I'll be a lot more stable, too."

"Oh, you'll get it," he said. "I have faith in you, and I'm willing to fight for you any way I can."

Slowly he pulled her gloves off and cradled her hands in his, sheltering them from the cold. Then he pulled the ring of emeralds and diamonds from his pocket. "I think you should go back to wearing this again. It looks good on you and I kind of like telling people you're my fiancée. I was thinking we could go back to my parents' house tonight. Then tomorrow, head to your sister's house for Christmas dinner."

She looked down at his fingers cradling hers. "I thought you didn't date and don't have time for a girlfriend."

"Who said anything about dating?" He slipped the ring over the tip of her third finger and let it hover there. "I'm asking you to become my wife."

Light danced in her eyes. "Trent Henry, are you actually trying to propose to me with a ring you found in a mud puddle at a truck stop?"

"Would it help to tell you that I followed proper procedure?" he asked. "I turned it in to local police, waited to see if anyone claimed it and when they didn't, I tried to trace its rightful owner. Then when I knew for sure it was mine, I gave it to you."

"All that for a mud puddle ring?" Her eyebrows rose.

"Darling, I had it appraised. This ring is worth what I make in six months."

"You mean it's real? All this time I've been wearing real diamonds and emeralds?"

She pulled back, as if the ring was on fire. He caught her hand.

"It is. And you threw it at me in the middle of a dingy grill in front of a bunch of criminals." He gently slid the ring over the tip of her finger again. "It is as real, special, exquisite and precious as the woman I am trying my best to propose to right now."

She pulled her hand away again and crossed her arms. "Really? That is your best?"

He groaned. Then he got down on one knee in the snow at her feet and took her left hand again. He held it firmly.

"Chloe Brant, you drive me crazy. You challenge me, aggravate me, inspire me and invigorate me, more than anyone I've ever met. I'm crazy about you. I'm in love with you. I promise I will do my best to protect you, respect you and always be the steady, dependable rock you can rely on. Right now, I'm kneeling before you in the dark, in the very cold and very wet snow, on Christmas Eve, asking you very nicely to marry me. So, please, my love, my partner, my favorite person on this planet…please put me out of my misery and tell me you'll marry me."

A smile brushed her lips and filled her eyes.

"I love you, Trent, even when you drive me crazy. And I will love you for the rest of my life."

"And you'll marry me, right?"

"Of course I'll marry you!"

"Good!" He slid the ring onto her finger. Then he lifted her up off the bench, swept her into his arms and kissed her. Somewhere in the distance, he was sure he could hear Third Line cheering and whooping, and spurring the crowd on to clap. But all he knew for sure, was that Chloe's hands were in his hair, her lips were kissing him back, his heart was filled with more joy than he'd ever imagined feeling and he was going to love the irresistible, irrepressible woman he held in his arms for the rest of his life.

* * * * *

If you enjoyed UNDERCOVER HOLIDAY FIANCÉE, look for these other books by Maggie K. Black:

KIDNAPPED AT CHRISTMAS
RESCUSE AT CEDAR LAKE
PROTECTIVE MEASURES

Dear Reader,

I can't believe this is the tenth book I've written for Love Inspired Suspense. Did you know that Chloe was in my very first one, *Killer Assignment*? She's the detective who interviews Katie.

I'm not sure which book is my favorite but I do know which book was the hardest: *Headline: Murder*. I was on my final draft when suddenly Trent and Chloe walked onto the page. They're definitely two of my very favorite characters. *Headline: Murder* would go on to inspire both the True North Bodyguard and True North Hero series.

While I got a lot of ideas for this book from the Citizen's Police Academy, I definitely took some liberties with police procedure to speed the story along. The hockey teams, colleges and sports center are fictional. But Bobcaygeon and Haliburton are both real and very beautiful small towns. The gangs and drugs are made up, too, and get their names from a very dangerous fish and mammal, and a rather harmless spider.

Thank you again to all my amazing readers who've gotten in touch with your thoughts and suggestions. The best place to reach me is on Twitter @MaggieKBlack or at www.maggiekblack.com.

I'm so thankful you're sharing this journey with me,
Maggie

Get 2 Free Books,

Plus 2 Free Gifts—

just for trying the Reader Service!

*When danger strikes at Christmastime,
K-9 FBI agents save the holidays and fall in love
in two exciting novellas!*

*Read on for a sneak preview of
A KILLER CHRISTMAS by Lenora Worth,
one of the riveting stories in
CLASSIFIED K-9 UNIT CHRISTMAS,
available December 2017 from Love Inspired Suspense!*

The full moon grinned down on her with a wintry smile. FBI Tactical K-9 Unit agent Nina Atkins held on to the leash and kept an eye on the big dog running with her. Sam loved being outside. The three-year-old K-9 rottweiler, a smart but gentle giant that specialized in cadaver detection, had no idea that most humans were terrified of him. Especially the criminal kind.

Tonight, however, they weren't looking for criminals. Nina was just out for a nice run and then home to a long, hot shower. Nina lived about twenty miles from downtown Billings, in a quaint town of Iris Rock. She loved going on these nightly runs through the quiet foothills.

"C'mon, Sam," Nina said now, her nose cold. "Just around the bend and then we'll cool down on the way home."

Sam woofed in response, comfortable in his own rich brown fur. But instead of moving on, the big dog came to an abrupt halt that almost threw Nina right over his broad body.

"Sam?"

The rottweiler glanced back at her with his work expression. What kind of scent had he picked up?

Then she heard something.

"I don't know anything. Please don't do this."

Female. Youngish voice. Scared and shaky.

Giving Sam a hand signal to stay quiet, Nina moved from the narrow gravel jogging path to the snow-covered woods, each footstep slow and calculated. Sam led the way, as quiet as a desert rat.

"I need the key. The senator said you'd give it to me."

Nina and Sam hid behind a copse of trees and dead brambles and watched the two figures a few yards away in an open spot.

A big, tall man was holding a gun on a young woman with long dark hair. The girl was sobbing and wringing her hands, palms up. Nina recognized that defensive move.

Was he going to shoot her?

Then Nina noticed something else.

A shallow open pit right behind the girl. Could that be a newly dug grave?

Don't miss
CLASSIFIED K-9 UNIT CHRISTMAS
by Lenora Worth and Terri Reed,
available wherever Love Inspired® Suspense books
and ebooks are sold.

www.LoveInspired.com

LISEXP1117